The Test And Turnaround

Brandy Lynette

ROYSTON
Publishing

BK Royston Publishing
P. O. Box 4321
Jeffersonville, IN 47131
502-802-5385
http://www.bkroystonpublishing.com
bkroystonpublishing@gmail.com

Cover Design: Aaron Williams – ajwilldesign.com
Back Cover Photo& MUA: Brittney Williams CEO & Founder of Bee 3 Beauty

ISBN-13: 978-1-951941-83-3

Printed in the United States of America

Dedication

To all those who are single, dating, or married.
This is a reminder to do the work! Know that
working on yourself and/or a relationship may not
be easy, but it is well worth the investment if you
truly hope to gain a return.

I hope that this book will help restore your faith,
your courage to try again, and your belief in how
wonderful you are through your heavenly father.

Acknowledgements

I'm definitely going to begin with the most sincerest and intense heartfelt thanks to God for gifting me with the ability and opportunity to complete this book. It is because of Him that I am fearfully and wonderfully made.

Next, I want to thank my mom and dad and my beautiful grandparents. Thank you for always being there for me! Words cannot express the gratitude and appreciation I feel for your lifelong love, prayers and support in my life. I love you dearly.

To my other set of parents, mom and dad Hatcher. Thank you for your love and prayers that I know covered the boys and me while journeying through our very own storms of life. We love you.

To my sisters, thank you Brianna and Brittney for reading my book and giving me the raw and real feedback I needed even when I didn't want to hear it. Thank you for your continued support and being my number one fans through my big and small projects. I love you ladies!

To my sisters Sarah and Rachel. Thank you for remaining loyal to our sisterhood, I love you!

Another great big thank you and shout out to my talented undoubtedly dope cousin and cover artist Aaron Williams.

Thank you cousin for so vividly understanding and displaying my vision for this book. I admire you so much!

To my editors, Dr. Tanya Bailey and Dr. Toetta Taul. I appreciate your honest feedback, support, and the time you invested in helping me to produce my very first novel.

Thank you, BK Publishing for taking on my project and for providing such thorough guidance on not only producing my first book but providing step by step instructions and understanding of what it takes to publish, publicize and promote a book.

To all of my close friends, Kristal Lee, Angelica Little, Aundrea Ward, and Frances Baxter, thank you!! Thank you for believing in me and pushing me even when I wavered in my thoughts of believing in my work and when I wanted to give up, you listened to my ideas, and pushed me to move forward.

Last but not at all least, to my boys, Gabriel, Brayden, and Christian Hatcher. You are undeniably so my motivation and drive to do everything that I do. I know you're always watching me and this is the very reason that I grind so hard. I not only want what's best for you, but I want to be the best for you. Thank you for loving mommy through the good, bad, beautiful, and ugly days. I love you more than you can even imagine. Together we stand and united we thrive. Let's continue to push forward because we got this!

Table of Contents

Introduction

Newlyweds Josiah and Aliyah Williams are extremely active and at the forefront of the music ministry of their mini-mega church, True Believers Non-Denomination Christian Fellowship Church. However, like any and everyone else in the church, they are far from perfect. In the beginning, they worked hard to maintain this perfect image in front of people to avoid disappointing those who look up to them. But even that gets old. The pressures of life and disappointments in their home have added yet another level of stress that almost brings them to their breaking point not only in their marriage but as individuals as well.

Both quickly realize they have broken areas in their lives that need to be mended individually before they can come together as one and be successful not only in ministry but also in their marriage and family situations.

It's often expected for the husband, as the head of the household, to keep things together and afloat in the home.

But what happens when the husband falls? What happens when the wife gets weak? How do you regain the strength to pull yourself up and pull things together?

Lies, past abuse, insecurities, and adulterous affairs, threaten the stability of their minds, family, witness, and future. This past year has been a true test of faith, character, and strength that cannot be skipped over, avoided, or ignored. Will Aliyah and Josiah become another statistic of failed marriages in the church, or will they make it to the end to experience some sort of turnaround that looks much better than the heat, disappointment, and turmoil that they are experiencing now?

Chapter 1
Meet My Man - Aliyah

Josiah sat in the large 1500 plus seat facility in the very spot he occupied every Wednesday for mid-week service, Thursday for choir and praise team rehearsal, Sunday during worship service and any other day there was a special service, rehearsal, or church meeting held. He was present. His seat was on the right-hand side of the pulpit on the big brown Hammond B-3 Organ, at least I think that's the brand that we have. Nevertheless, my man was at his post. Faithfully devoted to his ministry, calling, and position, Josiah loved working as the minister of music at True Believers Non-Denomination Christian Fellowship Church. That's a mouthful I know, but we love our church.

TBNDC Fellowship Church was where Pastor Eric L. Blackwell resided as pastor. His wife, First Lady Crystal Elaine Blackwell, was Pastor Blackwell's right hand. She operated more along the lines as a co-pastor rather than first lady. Pastor Blackwell was never ashamed to let that be known. He'd announce it loud and proud to anyone who questioned his wife's position in the church. He wasn't old fashioned in believing that a woman couldn't hold a title as pastor. In his church especially, he recognized he was too busy to do it all by himself. So, they shared a partnership in marriage and in ministry. As a result, their ministry and marriage were beyond blessed! First Lady stood by Pastor Blackwell's side, not behind him, not in front of him, but right by his side. These two were a dynamic duo. A true force to be reckoned with. The Blackwell's were strong, God-fearing, loving, caring, innovative, and all-inclusive leaders of the 1500 plus member church located in Pasadena, CA.

Both Pastor and First Lady Blackwell were influential in Josiah's life and they loved him like a son. Once Josiah and I were married, they accepted me as a daughter as well. I'm not really traditional, and I definitely don't follow any strict hard-core formalities from any religious groups or organizations. Now, don't get me wrong, to each his own. I'm not knocking anyone choosing to live by an old school regime. I'm just saying, it ain't me. That's all.

Our church TBNDC Fellowship was not traditional in the slightest. In fact, the praise team members often wore shorts and jeans on Sundays during regular worship service, as did the Pastor when he preached. However, we weren't strangers to a good ole fashioned Pentecostal style service and holy dance. Most commonly known as "shouting."

Listen, I could cut a rug with some of the best of them. But at the same time, I was from that new generation of millennials that didn't necessarily believe that I shouldn't be allowed to wear pants, lip stick, or short sleeved blouses and if I did, the Lord surely wouldn't shun me for coming as I am. I even enjoyed an occasional glass of wine every now and then.

Don't close the book on me just yet, keep reading. I'm going somewhere with this. Anyway, that's a little bit of background on me and the handsome, talented, anointed, gifted in leadership, bold and fearless man of God that I call my husband. That six-foot tall, dark chocolate, slender athletically built, curly haired, black Jesus stole my heart over eight years ago, and I never desired to take it back. That is after I finally learned my value and was able to accept who I was created to be.

It wasn't just Josiah's gorgeous looks that made him captivating. The man was a naturally anointed and appointed leader, that hands down, was sexy as hell. There were days when he would be up there playing the organ so skillfully and brilliantly, and all I could do was picture all of the nasty, raunchy and dirty things I wanted to do to that man the minute we got home. That is of course, if we could make it that far because the car was always an option. God thank you for giving me this gift of a man! He was such a beautiful creation. There was no doubt about it, I was most definitely smitten with him. The funny thing about it is, in the beginning, not everyone including my husband could tell just how in love I was, and I wasn't always able to speak this freely about the man that I loved either.

Now, I know this is probably hard to believe or understand, but I promise you, I tell you no lies. The Lord sent me a man after His own heart, who loved Him unconditionally, and wasn't afraid to tell the world exactly what he stood for. I am a strong believer that because of this very reason, Josiah wasn't afraid to show and tell the world just how much he loved me, Aliyah Ariyanna Monet' Spencer.

I have to be all the way honest. Josiah's bold proclamation of love for me, at one point in time, intimidated the hell out of me. Eventually I learned that it was because I had not yet accepted me for who I was. Recognizing my self-worth, wasn't something that came naturally. In fact, I hated receiving too much attention and I was afraid to do any and everything. Because guess what, I knew if people got too close, or examined me for too long, then they'd eventually see my flaws. They'd catch on and uncover all of my imperfections that I so cleverly and beautifully covered up with my makeup, full body undergarment shapewear, outlet clearance rack clothing, swap meet high heels, fake nails, and occasional weave, braids or lace frontal wigs. Not to mention those stretch marks from excess weight gain when I had Josiah Jr. that I intentionally covered. I'd managed to shed some of the additional weight fairly quickly, but quite a bit of it still remained, along with the sagging skin in certain areas from all the years of wear and tear.

In spite of it all, I could pull it together if, and when, I needed to. Even when I wasn't feeling my best, you'd never know it. The thing is, I could find so many things wrong with me without people even asking me to. I didn't need any assistance breaking me down. I could run down a full lengthy list of my own shortcomings.

Unfortunately, I tended to devote too much of my attention to those flaws. I actually did have a pretty decent singing voice and could hold my own if need be. Now, I wasn't Dorinda Clark Cole or Kim Burrell by a long shot and I'm well aware that no one asked me to be, but I didn't want anyone to hear how far off from those two gospel legends I was. So, I opted not to sing alone and definitely not out loud to where anyone could hear me. I chose to keep it to myself.

Yes, one of the many gifts that God gifted me to share with the world, I chose to keep to myself. That was me, intimidated and afraid to step out, and intimidated and afraid to sit still. Crazy I know, but we all have our issues. So, there you have it. I've run through a long list of flaws that you didn't need to know about me, but now you know. If it gets out, I'll know you told.

The crazy thing about all of this is Josiah didn't seem to be bothered whatsoever by any of these imperfections that I listed. This man loved me anyhow and any way that I came, and that my friends, didn't make a bit of sense to me.

So, really listen when I tell you that this type of "stinking thinking" is exactly what caused the catastrophic break and tearing up of not only our marriage, but us as individuals as well. That's why it's always important to have faith even in the things you've never imagined, or believed could be true for yourself. The word of God is true when it says, "For nothing will be impossible with God." Luke 1:37. The thing is, I unfortunately had to travel a long hard road just to understand what that specific scripture really meant and how it applied to my life's story.

Chapter 2
This Thing Called Marriage - Josiah

Ok, let me just start from the beginning. Or no, I'll take you back a few years ago right before me and Liyah's true test and assignment began. It was a Thursday night. I sat positioned on the keyboard in the rehearsal hall while all the other praise team members of TBNDC Fellowship exited. We'd just finished the dismissal prayer of our young adult praise team rehearsal. I'm not one to be braggadocios, but tonight. . . man. . . tonight was lit! Every part was crisp and on point. From the band to the praise team members. Each member was "hittin'." Including my altos. Not to put them on blast, but they always seemed to struggle the most. Yo, tonight, I got chills. That's the type of rehearsal I love and it keeps me coming back and excited about doing my job.

TBNDC Fellowship was a pretty mixed congregation of African Americans, Caucasians, Pacific Islanders, Asians and Hispanics. As a result, our Praise and Worship Team was blended as well. Since we held auditions in order to participate in any area of our music ministry, we had some strong talented singers that sang with a lot of well-known secular and gospel artists in the music industry.

As each person exited the rehearsal hall, one of the praise team members yelled over to me saying, "Alright man, don't stay too late. Rehearsal was good as always!"

I responded with, "Yeah, we'll work more on that change on Sunday before service. Be blessed my dude."

A few other members offered their goodnights as well while I continued playing the chords to my medley over and over again. I just couldn't shake the anointing that rested so heavily in the room at that very moment. The spirit was thick, and I loved any opportunity where I could rest in the presence of the Lord in that manner.

Anyway, Tiffeny Cook, one of our strongest members on the Praise and Worship Team, stuck around after the crowd had cleared and conspicuously continued to pace back and forth in front of the stage where I was seated on the keyboard. But for what? I wasn't really sure, and I was too zoned-out to really even give it much thought. After pacing the floor several times back and forth and I guess calling my name several times, she finally became frustrated and decided to scream my name at full voice to get my attention.

"JOSIAH," Tiffeny exclaimed.

Clearing her throat, she shifted her stance, folded her arms with a sassy smirk on her face and piercing gaze in my direction, she asked, "Would you like for me to wait for you?" Tiffeny paused briefly, but not long enough for me to squeeze in a response.

"It's kind of late. I think it would be safer if we walked out together. Ya know," she finished.

Finally, snapping out of my music comatose to tune into what Tiffeny was saying, I responded, "Huh?"

I heard her, but I don't think I was really listening as I still had the next set of chords racing through my mind. I was ready to move into my next phase on keys until she repeated herself.

Tiffeny repeated her statement with a head nod and gesture pointing to her watch as if to say, it's getting late and perhaps I hadn't noticed.

With little to no hesitation, I responded to her, "Nahhh, sis. Go ahead. I'm good. I'll be wrapping things up shortly."

During that brief conversation, I never stopped softly playing my medley because I was so enveloped by the sound of music and worship that remained in the atmosphere.

"Be sure to run and catch up with the others so that you're

not out in the parking lot alone. I'll be about 5-10 minutes behind you. I still have to lock up. And thanks for coming out. You rocked it tonight, girl," Tiffeny blushed.

"Thank you, Josiah. That means a lot coming from a musical genius as yourself."

I just smiled and nodded a farewell to her. Tiffeny excitedly exited the sanctuary. As I sat on the organ, I transitioned into playing a lovely rendition and compilation of *Lord I'm Available to You* and *I Surrender All*. Both songs always seemed to pull me into a close intimate place with the Lord. I know I was supposed to be wrapping things up, but music was my release. It was my safe haven and comfort place. If there was ever a time that I couldn't think or found myself frustrated from life and its many challenges or heavy burdens, I would sit, play and sing, though, not just gospel music.

I was a lover of all types of music. I was raised on gospel because we attended church semi-regularly with my mom back in the day. When my mom realized how much I loved piano, she hired an affordable piano instructor who taught me classical music. How my mom came up with the money to pay for these lessons, I'll never know. So classical was my main base foundation.

As I grew older, I found that I definitely had a love for country and blues as well. But jazz, man, jazz, it's hard to describe it. Let's just say we have a romantic relationship and connection like no other. I was finishing up the last few bars, when my phone rang. It was Aliyah.

"Hey baby," I answered.

"Ok, Liyah baby calm down. I'm still here, but I'm headed out now. I realize it's 10:30 pm. I am wrapping up and headed home to you. Can you stop fussing so much please? Ok. . . I'm locking up now."

While listening to her complain about a few things she needed for the house, I tried to remain calm although I don't think I'd ever understand how anyone could be that passionate and argumentative over plugins, Tide detergent and bread. We needed it, ok! But, dang. However, if it was that serious to my baby, it was that serious to me.

I got up and began powering off all of the equipment in the rehearsal hall.

"Wait, what? You started off fussing about me not being home, but now you're asking me to go by the store. I thought you just said it's too late for me to be out, Liyah? And especially at Walmart. You know I don't like to fool with that store during the day, let alone late at night." I paused as she continued her ranting and raving.

"Ok, baby. Whatever you need. I'll go get it. I'll be there shortly. Calm down beautiful. I'll see you soon. Ok, I love you. . . Aliyah, I said I love you. . . ok, bye."

The next day, I stood in the kitchen making our son Josiah some *Eggo* waffles for breakfast. Our kitchen wasn't small, but it wasn't large either. We lived in Glendale, CA. This was about six to nine miles from Pasadena where the church was located. We couldn't afford to live in Old Town Pasadena like the Blackwell's, but with Liyah's income and me being paid generously enough from the church and other music gigs on the side, we could afford to rent a decent two-bedroom two-bath condo in Glendale. I loved the open floor plan in our home because it made it seem so spacious. However, when you're occupying space with someone who always seemed to not want you around, even an open spacious condo can seem way too crowded. I was pouring Josiah a small glass of apple juice when Aliyah walked in. She seemed to be in a mood. Although, I'll be honest, she seemed to be in a mood on a regular day to day basis. I couldn't help but to wonder if it was me. I will say that I noticed this seemed to come about after we married and when our son Josiah was born. He's two now. I know having our son was supposed to be one of the happiest seasons in our lives, but if I'm all the way honest, that season of our marriage during Liyah's pregnancy added another level of pressure on our marriage that weighed us down tremendously. It was to the point that instead of binding us together, we somehow drifted further apart. We were now functioning on auto-pilot barely holding on to our marriage by a thread. Don't get me wrong though, I loved my wife. It was just difficult.

"Are you taking Josiah to daycare this morning, or am I?" Liyah asked sharply.

"I will. I told you that I would last night." I responded in the best calm and even-tempered tone that I could muster up. I was sick of her talking to me like everything about me including my very existence irritated her.

"I was only asking because you weren't dressed yet and you seem to be taking your precious time with moving and doing things this morning," she retorted in this condescending tone that she so regularly took with me, that stayed pissing me off.

"Liyah, I said I got it. Don't start."

I walked out of the kitchen to go and put my clothes on, gather little Josiah's items for daycare so that I could get out of there and avoid any further unnecessary argument with Liyah. I swear it seemed like she intentionally picked fights with me just to have an excuse for us not to talk or be around each other. She stayed making comments about how we can't seem to get along and probably shouldn't be together. Listen, I understood the scripture that, "Love is patient, love is kind. It does not envy, does not boast, and is not proud. It is not rude, not self-seeking, not easily angered, and it keeps no record of wrongs." That's 1 Corinthians 13:1.

But Yo. . . let's be real. I don't care who it is, hell, even Jesus would have gotten tired of this foolishness Liyah was dishing out.

Normally, I would dismiss that crap she always brought up about leaving me because I knew what I wanted. But, lately, I was seriously beginning to question what in the hell we were still doing together.

Chapter 3
Inadequate & Insecure – Aliyah

I sat in a daze at work in my small cubicle area, which some called an office space depending on who you asked, replaying the conversation Josiah and I had this morning. Luckily our office was quiet because things tend to mellow out on Friday afternoons. I guess people aren't really in the mood to talk about their delinquent mortgage payments when they're entering into the weekend.

Listen, I definitely wasn't complaining. Being the Senior Foreclosure Prevention Specialist, my days stayed jam packed with stress and pressure as I worked tirelessly to reduce the number of foreclosures our company processed and increase retention rates for homeowners to keep possession of their property. I'm doing all of this for people who ninety-eight percent of the time only wanted to argue with me or just flat out curse me out. They stayed on defense about their stressful and humiliating predicament that was always somebody else's fault and never their own.

Customer service made up more than half of my regular day to day job responsibilities. Half of the time I wasn't in the mood for the foolishness, but I took it. The downside of it was, when I went home, I would unload all of the pinned up anger, stress, and frustration from work onto my family. Knowing that, weighed me down too.

I knew I'd snapped on Josiah unnecessarily that morning and every time I did that type of stuff, I immediately felt remorse when the words left my lips. I could see the hurt and anger in his eyes, but I couldn't stop myself. Yes, I say every time because it's happened more than once. In fact, it was becoming a regular with me. I was always so irritable.

At first, I wasn't sure why. Then, I realized one day that I just wasn't happy. How could I not be happy? Here I was with this handsome, anointed, and talented man, who from day one, loved me and wooed me. He showed me how smitten he was and never stopped pursuing me.

I met Josiah five years ago at a young adult conference when I was visiting True Believers Non-Denomination Christian Fellowship Church. I was singing with one of the choirs performing during the kick-off concert for the event. I remember thinking when my friend Cammie and I pulled up, "My goodness this church is huge." I will say the membership has grown a lot since my first visit to the church, but the ministry always seemed like a giant in my eyes.

I'll never forget when I spotted Josiah. He looked so handsome standing up there in the pulpit as the master of ceremony that night. He didn't hold his title of minister of music back then, but it was obvious that it was soon coming when he first opened his mouth to sing.

My GOD! That man's voice was smooth like silk. He had this calming tone about his voice and his runs were beautiful. He made crisp riffs and although his tone was soft, he could go hard once the Holy Spirit got a hold of him. He would go in like full beast mode.

This man's vocal range was out of control. Josiah was nothing to fool with. His vocal style, a bit difficult to describe, was a mixture of Marvin Winans and Zacardi Cortez. You could tell the anointing was on him heavy because as soon as he got going, folk would start hollering instantly being slain in the spirit left and right.

I will say, I think half the women hollering may have only been to get his attention. Somehow, they would so conveniently run up and down the isles shouting and falling down right in front of him so that he could get a glimpse of how saved and holy they were. It was either that, or so Josiah could get a sneak peak of what it looks like when their skirts came up.

Anyway, I bumped into Josiah backstage after our choir had sung. We ended up singing a song that I lead, Ricky Dillard's *Amazing*. You talk about intimidating. I thought I was going to pass out the minute our director called me to the front. I may have mentioned it before, but although I had a voice, I wasn't comfortable with singing the lead. I thought I was going to black out, choke, pee, cry and die all at the same time. My throat always dried up when I had to sing in front of people. My nervous system worked against me during times like these. It was really sad because I absolutely loved music.

That night, I got through it and it went well. I ran off the stage before everyone else because our Director had decided to go back in to the chorus one last time. He'd decided to fill in on the lead because I'd already taken my exit. You know church folk always get excited, as we should, when we start talking about the goodness of the Lord. I'd almost made it back to the hospitality room when I bumped into Josiah. I hit him so hard it knocked the wind out of me. Yes, that's how fast I was moving. Plus, my head was down, and I was still a bit emotional from the song I'd just sang with the choir.

God is really good and anytime I thought of His goodness, it would get me going. I almost fell from the collision with

Josiah, but he grabbed a hold of me and pulled me in toward him. When I looked up and realized I was being held by the one and only Minister Josiah Zachariah Williams, my nerves began to really spiral out of control.

He smiled and said, "I'm sorry sis. Are you ok?"

I stuttered and attempted to respond, but nothing came out. Actually, something came out, but it sounded like a broken hello and a hiya ba-ba-ta, like I was speaking in plain English and holy tongues both at the same time.

He smiled again, "Boy STOP!" I screamed in my head. Between his smile and my emotional high from the Holy Spirit, I was completely discombobulated. If he kept flashing those pearly whites at me, I don't think I would have ever regained the strength I needed in my knees to stand up straight on my own.

While still holding on to me, Josiah said, "Well. . . I gotta head back out there. Be careful ok."

I finally regained control of my motor cortex to send a signal to the frontal lobe of my brain and was able to say, "Ok. I'm so sorry, please forgive me. . . go ahead."

We both laughed at our clumsy encounter, let go of one

another, and parted ways.

Before he moved too far away, Josiah turned back and said, "Oh, by the way, I enjoyed you up there. You have a beautiful voice."

And just that quick, he turned back around and ran out to return to the stage. Me? I stood there stuck for what seemed like an hour trying to wrap my head around what he'd just said. Did Minister Josiah really just compliment me? Needless to say, I was definitely speechless. What a night.

The next week following the concert, I logged into my *Facebook* account to find a pending friend request from the new age black Jesus himself, Minister Josiah Zachariah Williams. I couldn't stop smiling as I stared at the request awaiting my approval. Call me crazy, but I honestly wasn't sure if I should accept it or not. Thank God I had my page set to private and people could only see the one picture I had set as my profile pic until I approved them as a friend.

I immediately began searching through my old photos on my profile page wondering what posts and pics I had on my timeline that he could scroll through and get turned off by. If he did, then he'd want to rescind his request.

Yes, all of that went racing through my head. So, I took my

time going through every single picture attached to my profile. I mean every single picture I posted, every single picture I was tagged in, and every comment I'd added to my page. I cleaned up my profile a lot. It was long overdue anyway, at least that's the excuse I used to help me feel better about the obsessive-compulsive neurotic behavior that I'd just displayed.

After tidying up my page, I still hadn't accepted the request yet. Next, I took a moment, well a day or two to take a few new selfies, with filters of course, to post on my page for all viewers to enjoy. I took a few with my huge white smile gleaming, and a few serious yet sexy but still saved pictures, for the top of my thread. Now, I was ready to accept his request.

Not long after I accepted his request, he'd sent me a direct message to apologize again for almost knocking me over at the conference the other day. If you could have seen me typing my reply. Listen, my cheeks hurt from blushing so hard.

"Good evening Minister Josiah. Please believe me when I say there is absolutely no need for you to apologize sir. I am actually the one who should be apologizing to you. Had I been paying more attention to where I was going, we would not have collided. So please. . . forgive me."

Josiah responded with, "LOL, I guess both of us could have been a bit more attentive to where we were going that night. But, it's all good. Really. I'm actually glad I bumped into you when I did. It gave me an opportunity to meet you."

Me, "Wow! I was just thinking the same thing. Had I not run into you, literally speaking, LOL...I might not have had any other opportunity or excuse to talk to you."

Josiah, "Yes, Ms. Aliyah. God's got a way of doing things. It is Ms. Right?"

Me, "He's definitely got a way of doing things and I like the way He do it. And yes, it is Ms." I continued blushing in total disbelief that I was actually having a DM conversation with this man.

Was he really asking me about my marital status? Does this mean he was interested in me? Or was he only asking because he wanted to make sure he wasn't overstepping somehow by sliding in another man's wife's DM.

Even with pure intentions, direct messaging through social media was always interpreted as a pickup regardless of who it was and, or what was said. I swear I hated social media sometimes. For someone like me who was always so nice and often times naïve, I stayed misinterpreting the rules of the social media game.

Anyway, Josiah went silent for what seemed like forever to me. I immediately became nervous and wondered had I said something wrong. Did I sound too desperate? Unholy? Had I forgotten to take a picture down from my page that he saw and became disinterested? I knew it was too good to be true.

Two days passed and finally a notification popped up on my screen that read, "New message from Young JZ Williams." Seeing the message immediately gave me butterflies, even his profile name was smooth.

Josiah, "Hey Ms. Liyah. Is it ok that I call you Liyah? How are things with you?"

Me, "Ummm. . . hi stranger. Of course, it's ok. I am well. I'm glad you hit me up." I wasn't sure if I should have added that last part about hearing from him, but against my better judgement, I did it anyway.

Josiah, "Cool Deal! I'm straight though. Things have been so busy with church and work and I had some family drama and pretty much just life in general. Other than that, I'm blessed and highly favored. Yo! I love your name. What's your full name, Ms. Liyah? That is, if you don't mind me asking."

Me, "Oh, I completely understand. Life is life and things happen. I'm glad to hear that you're doing well. My full name is Aliyah Ariyanna Spencer."

Josiah, "Wow, I love it! So, Ms. Spencer. I'm not normally this forward, but I feel lead to ask you out on a date. Would you be interested in going out to dinner?"

Me, "ABSOLUTELY!" I thought about it after and realized the all caps and multiple exclamation marks may have been a bit much and come across anxious, but oh well, I couldn't take it back now.

Josiah, "Cool, may I have your phone number? I'll text you the details so that you have it in writing."

I wasted zero time providing him my info. I did, however, instantly become nervous and intimidated. I began to do what I did best, question why he was asking me out.

What was it about me that sparked Josiah's interest? This man was handsome, talented, anointed and well-respected in the church and community. What the heck would he want with me?

Honestly, I didn't believe that I was ugly or unattractive, but I knew I had my flaws. I was wearing braids at the moment trying to regrow my hair since I'd cut it and colored it so much, it was pretty damaged. If he knew that, would he still want to talk to me.

I wasn't the skinniest or healthiest person either. Now, I wouldn't have classified myself as pure ole fat, but I was what a lot of my friends often referred to as "thicker than a snicker." Honestly, I don't know where people come up with these sayings. Always comparing big people to food, which was not helping my self-esteem in any way, shape, or form.

I was what many people would call shapely. This was true. Your girl had plenty of curves. If you were to ask my opinion though, I would tell you it was way too many curves. Enough curves to make a man get motion sickness if he stared too long. I'd realized after, that perhaps I responded prematurely in accepting his invitation to go out on a date.

I had no business going out with or even talking to a man of this caliber. I'd wait until tomorrow, but I definitely planned to send him a message to cancel these plans to go out with him. I know this sounds disturbing. A few of my friends even suggested that I maybe suffered from the imposter syndrome.

***

After a few attempts to turn down that date with Josiah and him refusing to accept "no" or I've changed my mind as a cop out, we ended up going out. If I'm completely honest, I've never been one to feel comfortable around any man.

Perhaps it had to do with the fact that my parents were divorced when I was a young girl. I don't even remember a time when they were together which resulted in me not spending a lot of time with my dad. Healthy relationships and love weren't something I saw. They were unfamiliar to me and seemed like a far-off unattainable fairytale for someone of my size, class, status and skin color.

According to societal standards, dark brown girls weren't exactly the pick of the litter. I would need a little more vanilla added to my melanin for attention from the opposite sex.

My brother and I lived with our mother primarily, so I never got a chance to establish a close-knit relationship with our father. In fact, he'd remarried, moved to another state and had an entirely new family. Money was tight, so we definitely couldn't go visit. Not to mention, his wife wasn't a fan of me or my brother, so we just let him move forward and live his new life pretending like it didn't bother us in the slightest.

However, the lasting negative implications my father's absence had on my brother Alex was painfully obvious. It was sad too. My brother was so handsome and talented. Women loved his swag. Alex knew it too. He stayed cheating on women, taking everything these women were willing to give, and moving on unbothered after he'd taken all he could take.

That was my brother. He knew I couldn't stand his treatment toward women and lack of value for relationships. Honestly, after seeing my dad's actions and now my brother, I didn't trust men or relationships and sure as hell didn't believe I could ever have one of those fairytale marriages.

Deep down, I did always wonder if having a loving marriage is something that could one day happen for me. Lord knows I didn't look like Becky with the good hair, and I was like hundreds and thousands of other Americans who lived paycheck to paycheck, so my financial status wasn't one built for that happily ever after lifestyle. In a nutshell, it was clear that I had my own personal insecurities and issues that prevented me from truly getting close with anyone.

I tended to guard myself. Rightfully so though. My mother

and all of her siblings were divorced. From what I can remember, they were all either disrespected or abandoned by men, or at least one of the aforementioned applied in all of their lives. Even my mom's mom was divorced. It was crazy.

Yet when I met Josiah, things were just different. Out of all of the men I dated, he was not only able to break down my wall of insecurity, he inspired me to believe in love and in me. He actually led me to believe I was worth love. I began to feel like I could actually be more than just everyone's go to only when they needed something. For a brief moment, I experienced what I can only describe as a transfer of confidence. Josiah had me believing that I could actually be a wife, someone's "good thang."

As days, weeks, and months passed, Josiah and I continued to date. We continued to grow closer and he eventually proposed. Josiah and I prayed with and for one another often. I loved that about him. He was sincere about his relationship with God.

I'd love to be able to say we remained celibate our entire courtship, but I dare not tell a lie. Something that's even more commendable is that once that line was crossed, Josiah didn't pull away from me. He pulled closer to me and shortly after proposed to me.

I dated a minister before Josiah. This guy actually took my virginity and shook. He said after what happened between us, he realized that I was a distraction and disruption in his spiritual walk with the Lord. He said God told him that our crossing the line of maintaining celibacy was his confirmation that I was clearly not the one for him.

This of course was the total opposite of the game he was spitting when he was trying get in my panties. I can't stand lying, cheating, and counterfeit clergymen using the Lord's name in vain to get the goodies from women. In, and/or out of the pulpit, men are still men. PERIOD! Anyway, I digress.

When Josiah told me he truly felt like the Lord was showing him that I could be the one and that he believed there was no other woman for him, I wanted to curse him out. Actually, I think I did curse him out. Sadly, it was because this wasn't something that I was used to. I was determined not to allow anyone else the opportunity to play with my emotions again.

Josiah was different like I said before. He reminded me daily that I was without a shadow of a doubt his "good thing." No matter how hard I immaturely tried to push him away, he never went anywhere. He showed me, not just told me that he honestly believed what he said about me being God sent. The issue, however, was getting me to believe it.

Chapter 4
Pressure Points – Josiah

The everyday routines of my life were beginning to become mundane, predictable, and unnerving. I swear it felt like it was time for a change. I was beginning to question everything that I was involved in and apart of especially my marriage. As the Minister of Music, I worked full-time at the church and went into the office every day. Monday through Sunday, rinse, fluff, fold, repeat.

Not that there wasn't anything exciting or interesting happening in the church because yawl know as well as I do, church folk will keep things interesting for you with all their drama and scandal. But, honestly, even all of that foolishness was getting tiresome.

Pastor Blackwell, who I actually refer to as dad, felt it was time for me to elevate my participation in ministry. He said the Lord revealed to him that I was ready to step into a position as Young Adult Pastor.

Maybe my ears were plugged, and perhaps I suffered from head congestion or something, but I definitely hadn't heard the Lord say that to me. Crazy thing about it, there were a few other ordained ministers five to ten years my senior, who wanted that position. These men were desperate for the title of Young Adult Pastor. In fact, they'd gotten wind that dad wanted me to step into that role and all hell broke loose.

Every day was some new rumor floating around about me. I may not be the sharpest tool in the shed, but I'm no fool. It's not a coincidence that as soon as the news got out about dad wanting me to take the young adult pastor's position, rumors start spreading that I'm gay, beating my wife and stealing from the church offering plate.

Man, I swear. Sometimes church folk seem to be the worst ones. These dudes stayed talking trash to me and reminding me how I wasn't ready for any responsibility and was too young to lead. Yet they called themselves leaders ordained by God in the church.

I guess when it came to something you wanted, ego always had a way of intervening and wreaking havoc. I remember when I was younger, I looked up to these dudes. I always thought they knew everything! They could preach circles around anyone. As I continued my path in the school of theology, the dynamics of our relationships changed.

I truly try to pay these fools no attention, but sometimes it's difficult, and a lot of it has to do with me not even understanding why they are hating on me so much. I haven't the slightest clue as to why my spiritual dad wants me to consider preaching anyway! If he only knew the truth about the insecurities and struggles I faced. The mere possibility of me getting a pastor's position has some people acting completely out of character. James 3:14-15 says, "But if you have bitter jealousy and selfish ambition in your hearts, do not boast and be false to the truth. This is not the wisdom that comes down from above, but is earthly, unspiritual, demonic."

That word is 100% flat out facts! If these so-called men of God could switch up on me that quick over the possibility of me becoming a pastor before they did, then it was evident they are undeniably serving the wrong Master. I hadn't even accepted the position yet! God only knows what they would try to do if I actually took the position.

One of these fools told me to stay in my lane and keep singing my pretty little songs like I do because after all, that's all the Lord called me to do. After I finished school, Minister Kenny showed up to my graduation and said, "Don't get too cocky with yourself son, and always remember the Lord only called you to be a song bird." This fool even made a chirping sound after he said it. His old ass swore he was a comedian.

Listen, I grew up in the church, but I was introduced to the rough side of the world at a young age because of the side of town I resided in. I say that to say, I didn't hesitate when it came down to me needing to whoop someone's ass. Fighting was how I made it through my journey back in the day, and knowing how to fight was necessary on a daily to avoid getting bullied and keeping all of my personal belongings.

Minister Kenny needed to be careful about coming for me the way that he did, because he was coming really close to catching more than the Holy Ghost at True Believers. He was getting really close to catching these hands.

Since I'd been at True Believers, I'd done pretty well with controlling my temper and growing spiritually. Typically, I would have cursed this Negro out long time ago and asked little man-man to catch me outside, but because of the Lord's saving grace, that hadn't happened.

It was evident the Lord was doing a true work in me. Back in the day, before I met Pastor Blackwell, people wondered how and why I carried on the way that I did with my temper and lackadaisical demeanor. I didn't care what title you held in the church. If you disrespected me, you could get it! Flat out!

When I was a kid, my biological dad wasn't home much because he worked a lot. A LOT, LOT! He was always out of town. Even when he was home though, he was drunk and appeared to be unhappy to be there with us. Some family members on my mom's side rumored that he had another family out of town somewhere. My momma never entertained the rumors, so, neither did I.

In fact, he was gone so much, life without him was normal to me and I was so used to his absence, that I didn't care enough to investigate where he was because it was awkward and sometimes uncomfortable when he was home. It was apparent to everyone including me and my blood sister, Trina, that momma was a single parent.

I love my dad, but our relationship just wasn't, and isn't there. At a young age, I had to step up at home and help my mom with bills and taking care of the house.

When folk tried to test me at school, I learned early that showing fear was a sure-fire way to get whooped. So, I fought back. I stayed in trouble though. In fact, I ended up not graduating high school because I was in trouble so much.

When I went to school, it seemed like I would get suspended or kicked out just for walking through the door. So, I quit school and started playing at a church full-time to get money and to help my momma pay bills at the house.

Of course, me dropping out of school wasn't something my momma necessarily agreed with, but I pretty much did what I felt was best. As a result, I think our roles got muddled, because I'd taken on so much responsibility at home that momma didn't even argue with me when I spoke up. She always said I was strong willed like my daddy, and it was like talking to a brick wall when trying to convince either of us to change our minds about something.

It wasn't until I turned 21 and was hired here at True Believers, that Pastor Blackwell found out I hadn't graduated high school. He noticed it on my employment application that I completed for the church. I was honest. In the past, there was never a reason to lie because I didn't need a high school diploma to play music. God had gifted me to minister through music to the masses even with a 10th grade level education.

But Pastor Blackwell wasn't having it. As part of my employment contract, I was required to sign-up for classes in an Adult Education High School Diploma program with the city of Pasadena while I worked at the church and earned income. The salary wasn't bad either. Not to mention, there was no cost for me to participate in the Adult Ed program. The agreement was, once I completed the program and obtained my diploma, I would no longer be considered a contractor, but I would become an official staff member, receive full benefits, and earn a five percent pay increase. To top it all off, at that point, I would be a high school graduate. It didn't seem like a bad idea to me, so, I took it.

After I finished the program, I figured it wouldn't hurt anything to continue going to school to learn the word of God more. After all, my whole life was church. I wanted to, and felt like I needed to understand it all. Blackwell took me under his wing from the moment I began working at his church. The Blackwell's had two biological children; one daughter and a son. Lorie was 32, and about six years my senior. Their son Leon was 28 years old.

The two of them were heavily involved in ministry in the church as well.

Lorie was over the children's ministry, while Leon was currently in class to become a minister. It took him a while to figure out his calling. Even now, he wasn't quite sure becoming a preacher was what he wanted to do, but he figured, "Why not?"

Both Leon and Lorie were married and had 2 children each. I loved those kids like they were my actual blood nieces and nephews. This was my spiritual family. I grew to love them dearly and we became extremely close. I still sent my mom and sister money on a regular and checked in on them, but because they lived so far, my time and holidays were generally spent with the Blackwells. This happened so much so, that when people came to the church, they thought I was truly a Blackwell. They only knew me as the Pastor's son.

Honestly, I looked up to my sister and brother, Lorie and Leon. I admired their commitment to the church, their families, and respected the overall family relationship dynamics they had with one another. When I was welcomed into their family, I immediately felt a part and figured, I too, could have what they had.

It gave me a hope I never knew and never considered having for myself concerning a family, a wife, children, and just flat out growing up. But, when I looked at them, I knew it was something I wanted. Although I was excited about the idea of having my own family like Lorie and Leon, I will say that I was somewhat intimidated. I didn't know the first thing about being a family man, other than what I witnessed recently with the Blackwells.

I grew up with my mom and sister in the home. Since my dad wasn't around much, I taught myself a lot of things I needed to know about manhood. Hell, I didn't even learn how to change a tire until I was older. Even then, Pastor Blackwell taught me that.

Leon and Lorie also had jobs outside of their positions within the church. So those two made good money. Even their spouses had decent jobs. Their families were well-off and carried themselves well.

I wasn't jealous of my bonus brother and sister by far. I just didn't know whether or not I honestly had what it took to carry a family like they did. I didn't grow up like they did. But, when I met Liyah, everything in me knew that I sure as hell wanted to try.

***

After I left home, I dropped off little Josiah at the daycare as promised.

I'm not gonna lie, I was irritated, and I couldn't focus on anything I was supposed to be doing for the church. My mind and heart were on Liyah.

Things just didn't feel right. Honestly, I wasn't sure what else I could do differently to improve our relationship. The scary thing about it was, I can't say that it felt like I was losing her. I felt like I wanted to leave her. This is one of the main reasons it had me freaking out. I'd put up with a lot and I do mean A LOT of stuff with Liyah, but lately, it was getting old. I was tired of being taken for granted and in her eyes, I couldn't do anything right. It seemed I just wasn't good enough for her.

Liyah had her master's degree in business marketing and I barely had a high school diploma. I don't know what I was thinking when approaching her. After we started dating, I learned that she was a couple of years older than me, and I could tell she was used to dating men who were more mature and more established than I was.

With the ambiguity of it all, between the new position being presented at church and my marriage, perhaps I needed to take some time alone to sort through some things to figure out what my next steps were.

Chapter 5
Temper Tantrum – Josiah

Sunday morning service was a prodigious experience. Dad's message was on point. He preached a sermon titled, "Keep your faith and your focus!" It was based off Isaiah 26:3-4, "You will keep in perfect peace all who trust in you, all whose thoughts are fixed on you!" My GOD that man preached today.

The choir sang *Perfect Peace* by the legendary Keith Pringle. That song always got to me. There is a section in the song that goes, "All belongs to Him who has made us. He watches me. So, why should I be bound when God has set me free." That part right there, alone, is packed with power. I realized I needed to stop allowing myself to drown in the worries of things that weren't even really a thing.

This is why it is important to avoid making permanent decisions based on temporary situations. I needed to take my mind and focus off of what I was worried about and meditate daily on what was real and concrete, which is God and His goodness. He was the greatest supplier of peace, "perfect peace" to be exact.

Dude, I was on a severe high after service. I felt a great release and felt like I was ready to go at life again another week, however, that was until church was over.

I went into the office to grab a few things before heading out. I'd left my bag in my office. It held some of my musical equipment. There was a great deal of equipment I kept at home instead of the church since I had a studio at the house. It was then that I ran into Ministers Kenny and Duncan.

First off, Duncan pushed passed me without offering up an "excuse me" or an apology. This Negro knew full well he bumped into me. Get this, he actually had a smirk on his face too when I looked up to see if he was really going to pretend as though he didn't owe me an apology.

That's when Kenny chimed in to say, "We enjoyed you today song bird."

I responded with, "Mannnnn, you got one more time to refer to me as a bird Kenny." The irritation was clear and evident in my tone at that point.

Duncan was in the back snickering and making bird chirping sounds. It truly amazed me how these dudes were close to a decade older than me and yet acted like they were ten years younger than I was. If I didn't know any better, I would think that perhaps they felt threatened by me in some way, shape, or form, but that didn't make any sense. Did it?

Kenny began in on me with, "Yea, we heard you tryna preach after your song today. You tryna prove to "daddy" that you are worth the Pastor position?" Duncan laughed to encourage Kenny's idiotic infantile behavior.

My response was to not respond. Liyah was waiting on me and I knew she'd probably been growing impatient and restless by now.

I moved to walk past Kenny when he got in my face and whispered so close that I could smell the coffee and cigarettes he'd obviously had earlier that day, "You tryna get close to me little birdie. I don't swing that way baby boy."

The South side of Chicago came out and before I knew it, I replied with, "You swear you don't like me Kenny yet you enjoy watching everything that I do. I'm beginning to understand now. You're a fan. No need to get this close for an autograph boo."

I took the pen off the table and signed my name in big ass font on his crisp white shirt underneath his suit coat. His nostrils flared so wide he probably could've sucked up all the furniture in the room had he inhaled too quickly. But had

Duncan not grabbed him, Kenny was about to catch all this smoke I was ready to bring.

If this fool really thought he was going to run up on me and instigate a fight and I wasn't going to deliver, mannnn, he had me all the way messed up. Duncan was holding Kenny back as he lost all his religion, lashing out at me verbally by calling me every derogatory term in the swearword dictionary.

He attempted to grab at me, and I walked past him without flinching once. I wasn't tryna bash Kenny's face in at the church and cause any embarrassment to my dad like that, so I walked off, but this old man surely had me mistaken if he thought I was going to run off scared.

Yo, he had me ALL THE WAY messed up. In an effort to de-escalate the situation, Duncan held Kenny back trying to calm him down. I presume it was to help him avoid getting his ass whooped. Whatever the case, I was straight.

As I made my way out of the office, I bumped into Tiffeny. She was all smiles all the time. Honestly, it was refreshing to see and receive something. . . something positive and unanticipated, yet necessary.

As she eased in closer to me, she gently touched me on the

shoulder and compassionately asked me if I was ok. I didn't disclose all the heaviness on my heart at that time, but it was refreshing just to hear and know that someone cared enough to even ask.

Tiffeny followed her question with an, "I enjoyed you today Minister Josiah," whispering softly in my ear.

She then asked how I was doing. Honestly, I couldn't even formulate a response to react to her bold words of affirmation.

I chose to respond with, "I'm coo sis. Thanks for asking. I'll hit you up later though to check in with you."

Tiffeny smiled a bright enthusiastic grin again and responded with, "Yes, please. Do that."

I walked over to where little Josiah and Liyah sat waiting impatiently. "Yes," I said impatiently.

By now you know Liyah wasn't waiting five minutes for me to use the bathroom without tripping. She rolled her eyes and immediately began complaining about my tardiness and inquiring as to what had taken me so long.

Annoyed and no longer able to maintain my always calm, cool and collective composure, I exploded with, "Liyah!

Don't start that bull-ish today!"

I somehow managed to refrain from using the actual curse word, "I'm not up for it right now. If you were ready to go, you should have asked your friend Cammie to take you home. I'm sure she wouldn't have minded."

Liyah looked at me side eyed clearly ready to fire back and cause an exciting scene at the church in from of all the "saints." These folks stayed ear hustling, itching, and waiting to have something to talk about. Before she could respond with her combative and contentious demeanor, her friend Cammie and my boys Aaron and Donte' walked up.

Cammie immediately started up in a light playful manner with Liyah and I while lifting Josiah yelling, "I'm taking my little man home with me if ya'll can't bring him to see me more regularly."

This was clearly done to create a diversion and direct others' attention away from my wife and me.

Aaron followed Cammie's lead by responding with, "Yeah, you two love birds always bickering over dumb stuff. What now? You can't decide whether or not you want chicken or fish for dinner? Ain't nooooobody got time for that!

Right lil dude?" Also talking to little Josiah.

Liyah however, still couldn't let it go. She rolled her eyes at the both of them then turned and asked Cammie if she could get a ride home.

To be honest, after she'd opened her mouth, I couldn't agree with her more. I didn't want her anywhere near my car because all I could think about was not only locking her out of my car, but running her ass over with it. The more I stayed with Liyah, the more it became painfully obvious that she flat out didn't have my back. It truly felt like I had zero support in every area of my life from her.

This was all beginning to be too much. I felt like I was suffocating. I get to the church and everyone needs me to be everywhere and do everything, and my dad keeps pressing me to be more involved in the ministry and do more in the church. As if I wasn't already doing enough! I was there seven damn days a week. I didn't know what else I could give! I was there at the church laboring, writing, singing, playing, giving, sharing, caring, praying, preaching and any other damn "ing" you could think of.

Not to mention I'm working hard to be this father to this little boy, this little dude who every time he looked at me it melted my heart and scared me all at the same time. I had no reference of how to be a good father to little Josiah. At the same time, I wanted to give him the world! What if I failed him as a father? I was already failing as a husband. I already knew that I wasn't that great at, or the most intuitive, on how to even be a man. All I'm saying is, I didn't sign up for none of this shit. For real.

Chapter 6
Unsolicited Advice – Aliyah

Josiah didn't realize, but I definitely saw Tiffeny all in his face at church yesterday. In fact, I always see her prancing and dancing around him. I couldn't stand her fake K-Michele wanna be thirsty THOT ass. She stayed in my husband's face, smiling and being all touchy feely with him. Yet, she couldn't even speak two words to me.

We could be right next to each other in church. Let the Pastor say turn to your neighbor and tell them you're glad to see them, Tiffeny's goofy ass would rush out before she was forced to lie to my face. I can't stand females like that.

Sometimes I really felt like I didn't belong in this "world." This church world I mean. The gospel music-land of public scandal, deceit, ego driven success, arrogance and backstabbing mess. Josiah had even told me when he and I first got together that his sister Lorie told him to be careful of me. I guess she didn't trust me or perhaps she didn't think I was good enough for her brother. Me and my over analytical mind took it to heart of course.

Back then, I immediately added it to my already existing list of reasons why I shouldn't have been dating or even considering marrying Josiah. My friends Cammie and Michelle would constantly tell me to stop talking crazy and accept my blessing.

Although my friend Michelle was usually the one who was always encouraging me to be with Josiah and to dismiss my "stinking thinking," Cammie always saw the way Tiffeny would hang around Josiah and didn't agree with Josiah and Tiffeny's behavior. In fact, she always kept me alert and aware of any inappropriate or suspicious activity between the two. After Sunday's encounter, Cammie was ready for me to officially put Josiah in the dog house.

It was funny though because Cammie didn't have a man herself. She couldn't keep a man because her mouth was too slick. At least that was what I always figured the issue was. Yet, my sweet and sassy single friend stayed offering her unsolicited advice on what I should do with my marriage. Normally, I wouldn't pay her suggestions too much attention, but I'm afraid today, she had a valid point.

Cammie and Michelle were both at my house that evening sitting at the dining room table with little Josiah while I stood in the kitchen cooking dinner. My plans that evening was to engage in intentional, entertaining and distracting conversation to keep my mind preoccupied with thoughts that didn't concern Josiah and Tiffeny. It appeared, however, Cammie had other plans.

Cammie continued to complain about Tiffeny and Josiah's close encounter, "That heifer swears she is fine. Just because she got a big booty, small waist, and can sing, Tiffeny thinks she is God's gift to men. It irks my nerves though because baby girl has so much confidence with so few edges! And sis is dumb as hell! Always walking around smiling with them crooked ass teeth. Why does she insist on flashing that $2.00 smile? Like, what the hell are you smiling for? Ughhh!"

I couldn't help but chuckle at that one. Cammie was crazy. A straight up fool.

Michelle chimed in with, "Well. . . she doesn't have no trouble pullin' men though, honey. In fact, she pulled your man, Cammie. But of course, that's why you're really mad ain't it?"

Cammie snapped back at Michelle, "Girl! Stop bringing up old stuff. I swear you love living in the past. That's why you always wearing those old played out pants. It's 2019 Michelle. Jesus Christ, step into today's fashion mommas. I don't know who you be expecting to pull with those old slacks you got from Walmart back in '99."

"Hold on now. Walmart be having some cute stuff now. Don't sleep on Wally World," I interjected.

"Key word, NOW! Walmart's clothes were not fly back in '99, they just recently got on the come up. Stop playin'," Cammie snapped back.

Michelle fired at Cammie with, "So you said all that to say what Cammie?"

"Stop bringing up old crap, Michelle. Put it to rest. I'm referring to the situation with my ex and that old-ass outfit you got on." Michelle rolled her eyes.

"Besides, I was planning on breaking up with Jonathan that day anyway! And yea, that is one of the very reasons I don't trust Tiffeny. She played me. She pretended to be my friend, calling me her god-sister, even tried to convince me to let her move in to my house, all while she was screwing my man. Nah Michelle, I haven't quite let that one go just yet. The Lord is still working on me." Cammie vented.

I tried consoling my friend by explaining that God was still good because He intervened early and revealed who Tiffeny and Jonathan were before things got too far. She was considering marrying that fool. God also allowed that situation to only last so long between Tiffeny and Jonathan. It was maybe two weeks after their relationship was exposed that Jonathan cheated on Tiffeny, ruined her credit, went upside her head, and then dropped her like a bad habit.

Cammie returned with her remarks of, "More like dropped her like a bad hobbit. I can't stand her ugly a..."

Michele interrupted her, "Cammie stop, now you know the girl ain't really that ugly."

Cammie's eyes shot in Michelle's direction appearing as if she was demanding Michelle to choose a side, now!

Michelle quickly understood and recoiled with, "Her insides are ugly and she ain't all dat! You right, friend. She ugly, friend!"

I couldn't do much other than laugh at the two of them. They stayed into it. It didn't take long for them to get back to me and my business.

Cammie quickly found her way back to me and asked, "What are you gonna do Liyah? You can't let this ride. She's probably already slept with Josiah by now."

Michelle cut her off once again, "Cammie! Stop! How dare you plant that seed!"

Cammie sounding somewhat remorseful from her choice of words, but still insistent on convincing me to take heed to her insight, continued with, "I'm just saying. You can't trust these hoes today. And we know full well Tiffeny isn't to be trusted with ANYTHING. Even if you don't leave him, I say make sure he knows he's in the dog house until he cuts all ties with her. In fact, he needs to make her leave the church!"

Michelle and I both exclaimed, "What!"

I replied, "Cammie, how do you expect Josiah to make that happen? He's not the Pastor. Plus, there is no proof that anything has happened. Just drop it. I don't want to talk about this anymore."

Cammie, "I know it's painful, but you need to figure out what you're going to do and quick before it spirals out of control. Trust no one!" Michelle sat quiet mostly as Cammie forced her unsolicited advice on why I should leave Josiah and whoop Tiffeny's ass. I must admit it did light a fire in me with or without any real proof of what had happened thus far. Finally, Michelle spoke. She always strived to be the more level headed and neutral friend. She was kind of like the glue that kept all three of us together because of her practicality and level-headedness.

Michelle spoke up and said, "Liyah, you know I love you. And I love Josiah. Cammie has a good point, but we also have to remember that she's been hurt in the past. So, she's speaking from a place of pain. Also consider, Cammie, nor I, are married. So, do you really want to take advice from your single friends? You can, but . . . tread lightly."

I could tell Michelle wasn't done speaking, but before she continued she paused for what seemed like forever. Perhaps it was to allow her time to search for the words she needed to say without hurting my feelings. There was maybe a three-minute pause before I looked in Michelle's eyes and said, "Go ahead. Say what you need to say."

Michelle finally spit it out. "I'm not married Liyah. So, I try not to involve myself in married folk business, but I think it's only right for me to make sure you're considering all sides of your situation right now, which includes your actions, friend."

I cut my eyes at Michelle unimpressed and somewhat offended by what she was implying. I was offended because, well. . . the truth hurts. "So, you're saying this is my fault,

Michelle?" I hissed.

Michelle responded hesitantly, "No Liyah. I'm just asking you to maybe put Tiffeny to the side and focus on Josiah. Why is he acting this way? Are ya'll having issues? Where do you and he fit in all of this that got you to this point?"

I couldn't respond. I simply bowed my head and fought back the tears that wanted to form with every ounce of pride left in my body. Cammie interrupted, "Well, regardless! Josiah made a vow to love Liyah through good, bad, rich or poor and sickness and in health. Bump that! He doesn't get to act like that because Liyah isn't perfect, he can just decide to step out! Hell naw, Michelle! He shouldn't have gotten married then. Uh hu. NOPE, I don't wanna hear that." Although I knew Michelle and Cammie both brought up valid points, I can't lie, I could only seem to focus on what was causing me my pain right then and there. Cammie's words had me shook, fired up and pissed! How dare Josiah cheat on me! I needed to confront him quick. As a matter of fact, he needed to get the hell out of my house and my life with the disrespect. I didn't deserve that. Right?

Chapter 7
Unsolicited Advice – Josiah

Aaron sat across from me at B-Dubbs while Donte' was next to me. We would often hit up Buffalo Wild Wings on a night when there was a game on.

This particular night it was the Heat vs the Magic. I wasn't crazy about either one of them, but if I had to choose, I guess I'd say Miami. Don't ask me why.

Perhaps it was because I like to play with fire at times.

Anyway, it was funny how my boys differed in opinions and character traits. Aaron was such a hard ass and showed no mercy with anyone. He spared zero feelings when he had something to share, even when it came to me. So, it came to no surprise how effortlessly and emotionlessly he slaughtered my wife Liyah that evening.

"Yo, that's exactly why I'm not getting married. These hoes ain't loyal. Chris Brown was preaching the whole-hearted gospel with that one."

Donte' chimed in with full frustration and irritation in his voice, "Dude. That's this nigga's wife you open and out right disrespecting right now. What's wrong with you fool?"

Aaron fired back as if he needed to remind me, "Aliyah doesn't respect you man. She clearly ain't happy and I don't trust her. All the stuff you've told us about how she be trippin' and you find her telling her momma stuff that's hurtful and she knows it is. Naw man... stop wasting your time on her. It's time to start over. What do you have to lose anyway?"

Donte' hollered, "Besides his family? Fool shut up! You sound real dumb right now."

"So! He can just get a divorce. It's 2019. Ain't nobody got time for that. Josiah, it's time to shake, rattle and roll my dude," released Aaron, un-phased by his surroundings or Donte's obvious disagreement and emotional rants.

"I would hope that you value your union before God more than that Josiah. I hear what Aaron is saying, and this of course is coming from someone who was hurt in a relationship before and has chosen not to allow time for healing. This is the thing, it's easy to just quit, and you most definitely can quit. But what if you stayed to truly find out the root of your problems and fight for your wife. For your son man! Don't you think little Josiah deserves to grow up with both of his parents in the home?"

I finally found something to say, "Not if we aren't happy. What kind of home is that for our son? All he's going to experience is bitterness and brokenness. How healthy is that?"

Aaron quickly co-signed on that one, "EXACTLY! That's all I've been saying."

Donte' looked at Aaron in disgust and replied with, "Naw, what you've been saying is don't work at things. Josiah, who said you will forever be broken or unhappy? It's up to you my dude to accept the healing and walk in it. But, real talk it's possible. Not to be all deep, but remember Ephesians 4:2, 'Be completely humble and gentle; be patient, bearing with one another in love.' It takes work Josiah."

Donte so easily explained as if things were really that simple. What he didn't understand was Liyah wasn't making an effort to work at saving us, and because of that, what's the purpose of me trying? If she didn't care, hell. . . why should I? Honestly, I loved my boys, but I hated when they involved themselves in my marriage. Neither one of these fools were married but swore they were experts on the topic. Donte had his nerve especially. He'd been married before. He and his wife divorced. I'm trying to understand how you all of a sudden become a strong active advocate for marriage

AFTER a divorce. Let him tell it, he'd do things differently if he had a chance to do it all over again. I hear him, but his situation isn't like mine and Liyah's. He just didn't understand. No one did and everyone really needed to mind their own business. I was in a class all on my own.

This frustrated me at times because I didn't have anyone I could turn to. Not anyone that wouldn't pass judgement. Pastor Blackwell would only show disappointment because I'm failing as a husband. His marriage was seemingly perfect, and he always knew how to respond.

I didn't have an example growing up. Plus, how would I sound letting the man I call Dad know that I was having second thoughts about the woman I swore I was madly in love with. He asked me on more than one occasion if I was sure about marrying Liyah. Plus, we'd had premarital sex. So, hell yea, I went to bat for my decision. Was my judgement clouded by that?

When I first laid eyes on Liyah, I honestly couldn't put what I was feeling into words. All I knew is I'd never met anyone like her before. She carried herself differently. It was odd because she had a timidness and confidence about her. Although Liyah always stood in the back, I could tell that she had not tapped into who she actually was yet. But I knew something wonderful was there and it was sexy as hell. I could see that there was a greatness about her, one I hadn't seen before in anyone.

Liyah was ALL THAT. Beautiful, sexy, educated, saved, talented and single. You could tell she had a strength about her too that read, "Don't approach me with the bullshit because you'll get your feelings hurt." It was that strength that would weed off weak men who weren't willing to risk being shut down because you could tell Liyah took no issue in saying "no" if she wasn't interested.

Till this day I'm not sure what gave me the confidence to even try talking to her because I don't do well with rejection AT ALL. My sister even told me once that I may have something called rejection sensitive dysphoria. She was joking of course, but now, I'm not so sure that it wasn't an accurate unofficial, uncredentialed diagnosis. It took a lot for me to open myself up to Aliyah, especially when I learned she had a degree, her own car, a good paying job and had already purchased a house. Man, she was only 23 when she bought her first property. And here I was a brotha who had barely obtained an high school diploma. Surely, she wanted someone more established with longer money than what I was carrying. I mean I could hold my own but holding "US" was something different.

Still, I couldn't let this opportunity pass me by. It's just I always wished I had an example growing up of how to do right by Liyah and little Josiah. I didn't have all the answers. I was praying, but something was blocking the responses. I wasn't quite sure what it was. All I knew is I surely wasn't trying to adhere to the unsolicited advice offered by my boys Aaron and Donte. They'd proven to not know a thing when it came to love, marriage or LIFE as far as I was concerned.

Chapter 8
Things Change – Josiah

I sat in the rehearsal hall outlining the praise and worship and choir materials for the week. I had to send them to the praise team, choir members and band. This Sunday was youth Sunday. I had my assistant director Tanicka teaching because I'd been asked to preach.

Man, let me tell you, I was not up for it. I just didn't feel it in my spirit.

Something wasn't right. I didn't feel worthy somehow. Liyah and I didn't have a bad week either. She seemed as though she was making a conscious effort to not pick fights with me, but I could tell she was still disconnected. It never felt like I had all of her. Physically she was present, but emotionally and even spiritually, she was somewhere else.

It was becoming more and more evident that I, Josiah Zachariah Williams, wasn't enough. Liyah deserved better. She deserved someone more educated, intellectual, and established.

As I sat there trying to fight the distracting thoughts of Liyah and conflicting condescending emotions I felt about having to preach on Sunday, Tiffeny walked in. She smelled like heaven too. I smelled her first before I could really see who it was approaching. She walked in with a big smile like she always wore. Her natural loose gorgeous curls were just as big as her smile. They looked soft and luxurious. Her hair alone could captivate anyone because you could tell she took the time to make sure her hair was healthy.

Tiffeny was a slim thick chic. She wasn't fat, but she wasn't skinny either. I wasn't one to have a preference on thin women. Something about a woman with some meat on her bones screamed grown ass woman. Listen, I was here for it!

Tiffeny walked up with her dark denim skinny jeans and high heeled boots that stopped at her ankles. I couldn't tell if she had on two shirts or if it was one with two pieces, but the top was cropped and cut up, and fell off her shoulders while she had a fitted tank underneath that hugged her waist, breasts, and hips. That outfit almost seemed strategically planned to snatch any man's attention.

I'm sure she wasn't checking for me. Tiffeny knew I was married, and she seemed like such a sweet girl. She was a few years younger than I was, but her confidence was through the roof. I loved that about her.

When she snatched the mic, she could shut the whole place down. This girl had mad talent. I'm not sure why she was single. Well, that was my presumption because I'd never seen her bring a man to church. Not that I was checking...or was I?

"What are you working on Minister Josiah?" Tiffeny cooed. Her voice felt like petals as the words fell on my ears.

"I'm attempting to send this material to Tanicka to teach during this week. I can't seem to get my mind focused. What are you doing up here?" I responded.

"Oh, I just stopped by to pick up some paperwork on help with housing from the bookstore. It's not for me though. I'd told a friend I would help her get established. She's starting over. She divorced her husband. They realized it just wasn't a fit. Neither one of them were happy, ya know."

She looked at me with inquisitive seductive eyes that captured my everything for a minute. I can't even tell you how long it took me to respond because I was so captivated in her gaze and taken aback by the information she'd just shared. As a matter of fact, I had no clue what to say next.

Tiffeny continued, "Anyway, I just want to be there for her as a friend. I'm proud of her though for starting over. She finally realized that some people are only meant to be in your life for a season and that was their reason. Nothing more and nothing less."

I finally snapped out of my trance. "I see. Well, I pray God's peace and comfort on her during this transition. I can't imagine that something like that is easy. You're not married are you Tiffeny?"

I have no clue why I asked that, but I did. I wanted to know. Tiffeny's smile seemed to grow even wider and she responded.

"No, Josiah. I am not. What would make you think I was? I've never been married, and I do not have any kids."

"Ok, well, you're still young, so that's perfect for the future Mr. Tiffeny." I smiled and stayed engaged to hear what she had to say next.

"Young? Well, there is a saying that I may be young, but I'm ready!" We both laughed.

"I heard that miss thang!"

"Naw, real talk. I prefer older men anyway. I'm tired of these young dudes that aren't about anything. They playing games and only looking to hook up sexually. I want more than that.

I have goals in life I'm trying to accomplish. I want to be married, established, build my singing career, and have a family."

She paused for a moment and followed with, "I'm not against blended families either." We both just smiled.

"Can I ask you a question Josiah?" Tiffeny finally sat down next to me to continue our conversation. "You seem to be disconnected lately. Are you good? Honestly, I worry about you a lot. I care about you."

I don't know what got into me, but I genuinely felt like she was telling the truth and I spoke up, "Honestly, things haven't been the best at home between Liyah and I. It just seems like we aren't connecting. We're not in a good place. I love her, but I'm not in love."

As soon as the words left my lips, I knew I'd said too much. Tiffeny sighed and seemed to be empathetic about my problems and place in life.

"It can happen Josiah. Just remember, you deserve to be happy. Any woman who can't respect you, value you, and hold you up as the man that you are, is a fool. You are a wonderful man and father!"

I interrupted her, "I'm flawed too Tiffeny. Nobody is perfect."

Tiffeny came back with, "Oh, believe me I know. I just want to make sure you're not allowing what you're going through to result in you losing yourself."

I had no words left. I couldn't even believe I was having this conversation with this single, never been married, talented, dangerous, six years younger than me female that I was clearly attracted to. She hugged me for a long time. She held me, yet it seemed like a genuine embrace with true concern for my well- being. All I knew was that it felt good as hell. The attention, affection, and adoration from that hug and encouragement was all long overdue.

The attention Tiffeny showed me at that moment made me feel like I truly was somebody and that I actually mattered.

When she finally released her hold on me, she followed it with, "I'm here for you Josiah. I told you before, text me or call me or...come by whenever or if ever you need to talk. I don't mind being your person if you need someone that will just listen and understand where you are and where you're coming from."

Her stare was so sincere. I pulled back and changed the

subject by asking her to go over this verse in a song I'd been working on. Let me tell you, that didn't help.

As soon as she started singing those lyrics while gazing directly into my eyes, it was over. My man Matthew said it best, "Watch and pray, that ye enter not into temptation: the spirit is willing, but the flesh is weak."

At that very moment, as Tiffeny was nearing the end of the verse with her velvet like voice and luscious full lips, I realized right then and there, I'd lost myself and was chartering into a new territory that was not only dangerous, but it unrelentingly held me captive in a place that I undoubtedly should not have ventured in to. It was then, that very moment that my mind, my spirit, and my emotions about everything truly changed.

Chapter 9
Hurt People, Hurt People – Aliyah

I laid in the bed next to Josiah not yet fully asleep when I felt his hand slide up my thigh and around my backside. Out of instinct, I cringed. Now before you get all upset and angry, begin calling me out of my name and say I'm wrong, let me finish telling the story.

Understand me when I say this, I LOVE my husband. I know I wasn't the best at always showing it, but I loved everything about him. From his talent, to his scent, his looks, his swag and style, even the way he mispronounced words when trying to sound extra intelligent, I loved him. Although I stayed correcting him, he didn't realize I still thought he was so cute because I knew he was trying. Yet intimacy, that was something else. It was something I'd always struggled with. It was also something I never spoke to anyone about, before or after marriage.

Many times, I was able to enjoy sexual encounters once I could block out the memories of the past. I would literally have to block the thoughts of feeling dirty out of my mind. That night in particular, I knew Josiah had felt me cringe at him touching and rubbing me, but all I could think about was her. I could vividly picture and hear her whispering in my ear, "Shhhh… You better not scream. If you say anything, no one is going to believe you because I'm going to tell your mom and everyone that it was your fault. You wanted me to touch you. You've been asking me to show you how to become a woman."

All of this said while she parted my legs and slipped her fingers in my underwear. She continued, "Stop pretending that you don't like it. Just lie back, relax and enjoy yourself. I know what I'm doing."

At eight years old, I had no clue who was right nor who was wrong. Crazy thing about it, I always hated being in that house. Even before the incident occurred. Everything about that place stunk, it reeked sadness, pain, torture, perversion, and death.

See, my mom was on drugs for a season. Yet, my brother and I loved her so much, that we desperately wanted to be with her wherever and however she was, even when it wasn't the safest or healthiest environments.

We moved to Los Angeles where my mom stayed with her close friend and drug buddy, Auntie Cee-Cee. She of course was not our biological aunt, but back in the day when adults were close friends, kids called them auntie or uncle even under circumstances when there was no real blood relation.

From what I could tell, Auntie Cee-Cee and all of her siblings were drug abusers. As a result, her 4 children had grown to mimic the same unhealthy lifestyle that mirrored their mothers. It was sad too, because her kids were only in middle and high school, but because of their environment they'd all picked up the injurious habit of drinking alcohol and using drugs. I honestly couldn't attest to what types of recreational drugs they'd become involved with because I was so young. All I knew is that I'd hear them talk about how fun it was.

For the most part, during our stay there, I tried to make the best of it. That was until that night. The experience took a part of me that I'm still not sure I'm able to put into words. There was an innocence lost.

Later in life when we began attending church and I learned about sins of homosexuality, I would cringe and wonder, would I be one of the ones falling for eternity for my past experiences. I didn't dare ask anyone, instead, I chose to block it. Block the memories, block the feelings and everything associated with it.

As I grew older, I picked up extra weight as a pre-teen. It stayed with me for years. It wasn't anything necessarily dangerous according to the doctors, but it was most definitely different and uncomfortable for me. I realized later that it was the weight of the incident that occurred that I continued to carry around with me.

I even grew to hate the place that the indecent exposure transpired. I viewed Los Angeles as dirty and dangerous. I vowed to never live there again. All the memories were negative. When I grew older, if anyone asked me about returning to live there, I screamed NO! I'd stay in surrounding cities but refused to do LA or anything close to it.

For a while though, I honestly forgot about the incident. I was able to forget to a certain extent. It wasn't until I married someone and I needed to share all of myself with him that I realized something was wrong. It was then that the weight became a problem. It was both a physical and emotional weight.

The requirements of me needing to be open and intimate and caring with someone else didn't come naturally and became extremely problematic for not only me, but him. Something was blocking that part of me. Things were tucked away so deep, that for a while I didn't realize the connection.

Josiah felt my cringe and uncomfortableness. He could always see the sadness in my eyes when he looked at me during times that we should have been happy and celebrating one another. He'd often ask me what was wrong. It frustrated him greatly because he believed himself to be the problem.

Majority of the time, I couldn't answer him because I didn't know the answer to that question myself. All I was able to recognize was that I wasn't happy. Something was missing. Not from him, but from me.

I felt so bad about cringing that night and other nights before that, I began to cry. I felt him quickly snatch his hand away, he rolled over, grabbed his pillow and left the room. I presume he went to sleep on the couch.

I laid there crying and holding myself. Carrying the physical, mental and emotional weight of being broken as a child all the way into my adult years and now my marriage was exhausting. I could tell that we, Josiah and I, were at the point of being broken as well.

All I could think to do was cry. Did I really know what was wrong? Even if I knew partly, I had no clue how to fix it.

There's something about recognizing mistakes while you're in it though, because Hebrews 12:15 would've really come in handy during this season of my life, "Look after each other so that none of you fails to receive the grace of God. Watch out that no poisonous root of bitterness grows up to trouble you, corrupting many."

It's a fact that hurt people, hurt people. In my marriage, we were a clear indication that brokenness begat brokenness.

Chapter 10
Backslide with Pride - Josiah

I was sick of it. I felt bad after I'd left the church that day connecting so closely with Tiffeny. So, I went home that night and tried to be intimate with my wife. I loved Liyah. I honestly did, but it was obvious the feeling wasn't mutual. Despite my irritation and frustration felt from my wife's rejection, the way that I was feeling had me ready for it. I wanted to make love to my wife.

Did it stem from the hot and heavy interaction with Tiffeny earlier that day you ask? Hell yeah! But, nonetheless, I had some built-up tension that needed to be released. At least I was trying to do it the right way, with my wife and keeping it in my marriage covenant.

We laid in the bed that night. I contemplated whether or not I should just let her sleep. But as I laid there, I couldn't get the nasty freaky thoughts out of my head. I wasn't big on porn and hell, I was married, I damn sure wasn't tryna have to pleasure myself when I had Liyah's fine ass laying there next to me.

I went in for the kill. I gently rubbed her thick thighs and moved the palm of my hand up to her round brown until she...she actually flinched. It wasn't like a "Oh, you startled me" type of flinch either. It was one of those, "Gross! Don't touch me" type of flinches.

I sat there for a minute to see if maybe I misinterpreted what had just happened. I even tried to ask what was wrong, but there was dead silence. She refused to respond. Needless to say, I lost my excitement. I got up and went to sleep on the couch.

After, I texted Tiffeny of course. It was a bold move I know, especially at that hour. But I noticed that she was up and online. Social media showed that she had coincidentally just liked one of my pictures on Facebook.

So, I sent her a text, "What are you doing up?"

Tiffeny responded of course with all these smile emoji faces. That girl stayed on an upbeat swing. I had to be honest, I loved that about her.

"Hey handsome! I took a nap earlier so now I'm up until who knows when. I hate when I do that, but I'm glad I'm up now because otherwise I might have missed this pleasant surprise position of Young Adult Pastor."

I smiled my damn self at that enticing response, but I didn't use any of those stupid emojis.

Instead I typed, "So what's your story Tiffeny? How do you stay so happy all the time? I love your energy girl."

Tiffeny took a minute to respond, but I could see the bubbles floating across the text thread, so I knew something was coming soon.

"I just realize nothing is really as bad as a lot of people make it seem. I'm blessed and I'm not afraid to go for what I want. Even if it's temporarily occupied by another being. I'm a go getter. I recognize that what God has for me, is for me. I also know that when I want something, I gotta work at getting it. Faith without works is dead, ya know? Me living by that motto has gotten me pretty far to date."

It took me a minute to take all of that in, but she had a good point. I know that I was one, oftentimes, who let people intimidate me by what I knew I was called and even had a desire to do, but because there is a possibility that it might offend someone else, I would tread lightly on moving forward with it.

Take the position of pastor for example. Why didn't I really want to do it?

Perhaps it's because I was worried about what other people would think. Not to get side tracked, but that's just a little about how I operate.

I responded to Tiffeny with, "That's what's up. I definitely want to get to that place where I could care less about what others think or feel about MY actions. I'm tired of living for everyone else. I need to live for me!"

Tiffeny with her smile emojis faces responded with, "Stick with me kid, I will take you places you have never seen before."

She followed that statement with a grin that made my excitement down under return. We both went silent for about five minutes. I wasn't sure what to say next especially since I knew I'd grown aroused by a comment that may or may not have meant what it sounded like.

I was getting ready to text a 'get some sleep' text when Tiffeny's next text popped up, "Hey, are you down to link up some time to go over some more music and talk more about releasing other people's thoughts about you."

I was ALWAYS down to go over music, hands down, but I doubt the church was where a connection like that needed to happen.

I said, "Bet! Let's play it by ear because I'm not sure where we can link up that would be comfortable for us and not cause chatter."

Tiffeny responded almost instantaneously with, "My house! I have equipment and a comfy couch for conversation. You know I dabble a little bit on keys."

Damnnnnnnnnn...is what I thought? This girl plays no games. She wasn't lying when she says she goes for hers. Plus, she can sing AND play keys. Wow, I can definitely dig that.

Although I knew our conversation was based around music and conversation on the cares of life, something inside of me screamed, "LIES!" Negro you know you tryna hit.

I of course ignored the inner thought in my conscious mind and said, "Let's do it. How's Wednesday night after bible study?"

Tiffeny smiled once more via text emoji and said, "I'll text you my address. Get some sleep. I look forward to going over music and more Siah."

She sent that text and immediately fired another text right after that read, "I'm so sorry, I just gave you a nickname. I got too comfortable. Is it ok that I call you that? It's a habit of mine always giving someone a nickname."

I responded with zero hesitation, "It's cool. I kinda like it. No one's ever called me that before so, it will be your special name for me. I'll have to come up with one for you too."

Tiffeny responded with, "Please do. I'd like that a lot. Rest up and I'll check on you tomorrow."

I shot back a text that read, "Goodnight Tiff."

She responded with, "I love it!" and a kiss face emoji. "Good Night, Siah."

My spiritual dad seemed to have been taking his precious time that Wednesday night during bible study. It felt as if it was dragging on forever. I'd even done my part by making sure praise and worship was cut short, but no, not dad. Blackwell had plenty to say that night. Ironically, his lesson was on playing with fire and getting burned. Proverbs 6:27-28, "Can a man scoop a flame into his lap and not have his clothes catch on fire? Can he walk on hot coals and not blister his feet? So, it is with the man who sleeps with another man's wife. He who embraces her will not go unpunished."

I can't lie, that spooked the hell out of me, but I'm not sure

Tiff was even listening to the lesson that night because she was texting me the entire time.

Asking me if I wanted to grab food, how she was excited about us being able to connect with no interruptions, and what time I thought I'd be there.

As much as I was excited about linking up with her, Dad Blackwell was tripping me out. Regardless, by the end of service, I shut all the equipment down on my end and headed out. I texted Tiff and let her know I'd be there in about 30 minutes to an hour. I wanted to check in with Liyah to make sure little Josiah didn't need anything at the house. I told her I had a session with some other vocalists on a project I was working on. Honestly, I don't think she cared really where I was, but just in case she felt like caring where I was that night, I needed to have my story ready.

I grabbed Tiff and I some food from this chicken joint that was not too far from her spot. I got the strips, fries, and a sprite, while she only asked for a medium fry and a sweet tea. All them potatoes was probably how she stayed slim thick. Yes, that immature and inappropriate thought crossed my mind as she told me her order on the phone.

I actually said it out loud and she laughed while responding, "Boy please, that's why I'm not tryna order too much. I gotta keep this figure right and tight. Slim thick is where it's gonna stay so I can be pleasing in thy site," she joked.

I couldn't help but laugh at that one. "Aiight, aiight. Well, pleasing it is."

I grabbed the order from the server and headed to her spot. When I got there, I sent a text to let her know I'd arrived and was parked right out front. As always, she came out wearing all smiles, of course, with some short shorts that showed EVERYTHING including the fact that she couldn't have been wearing any panties, with a tank top that hugged her body in all the right places. She'd thrown on some little flip flops that showed off her cute tiny pedicured toes.

I handed her the drinks, and immediately smelled her soft sweet fragrance that smelled like soft lavender and honey. I tried to control my manhood from losing control before we'd even made it to the door. "Down boy," I said to myself.

This girl was ALL THAT, but I asked myself what in tarnation I was doing here. I'd come too far now, there was no turning back. At least that's the lie I'd told myself to keep going forward. Romans 3:23 reads, "For all have sinned and fall short of the glory of God."

Right? A lot of people read that passage and stop there.

Because we all sin right, no one is perfect. It's just what we do. During that season of my life, I stopped there in the scripture. I only needed that much to get through. This type of reasoning helped me rationalize why no one could pass judgement on me for my actions, regardless of how wrong they were. So, you stop there in the scripture.

Perhaps I should have read on.

Chapter 11
A House Divided – Aliyah

As the days passed, it was evident to us and everyone that was connected to us that Josiah and I were drifting further and further apart. Sadly, I could see it, I could taste it, I could smell it and I could damn sure feel it. I could sense it all as it unfolded before my very eyes. Every fiber in my body was aware of the destruction of my marriage, friendship and relationship with Josiah Zacariah Williams.

I sat back and watched and pouted and even argued as it began deteriorating. Yet, I couldn't change it. I couldn't figure out how to turn it around. Deep down, he had to understand that I didn't want things to be this way. In the midst of trying to understand all that was going wrong with that relationship, I was still hurting over me. For that very reason, I became angry that Josiah couldn't see that. He simply didn't understand that I needed help. I was drowning to the point that I couldn't even cry out to anyone for help.

It seemed as well that because my emotions, attention, feelings and time was so wrapped up in my issues, that Josiah grew more and more heated and annoyed with me. This season of our emotional separation and disconnect lasted for approximately six months before Josiah finally told me he was moving out and needed his own space.

He sat me down as I held little Josiah in my arms and explained that he and I had grown apart. He continued by telling me that he loved me but was no longer in love with me. Josiah even tried to give me the "It's not you, it's me" spill to avoid any additional damage to my bruised ego and emotions, but I wouldn't allow that when he told me how he accepted.

I cut him off. There was no need for him to lie. I was fully aware that I'd played a role in the destruction of our current situation. When I asked if he was going to live with Tiffeny, he didn't respond. Now, I'm not stupid. I was aware along with everyone else at the church of the rumors concerning his infidelity. I noticed him coming home late months ago, the scent of a woman on his clothes tinged with alcohol.

Surprisingly, I'd never known Josiah to be a drinker, but he seemed to be drinking on a regular now, especially those nights that he came home late. When I say late, I mean 3-4 or sometimes 6 in the morning. He would be stumbling and fumbling over things when coming home. He'd even wrecked the car a few times.

The confusing thing about all of this was if he was happy with this new mistress, why was he drinking? What was he trying to numb and avoid by masking things with his new habit of drinking alcohol? He still held his position at the church, but his demeanor and investment spiritually, physically and emotionally were completely different.

From my understanding, Dad Blackwell tried on several occasions to talk with him to find out what he was dealing with, but Josiah wasn't a talker. He could be very private and prideful. That's why I was surprised when he accepted the help to get his high school diploma through the adult education program.

Typically, he didn't even talk about how he never got a diploma, nor did he share that area concerning his life with anyone. Pastor Blackwell only found out about him not having his diploma because he was paying attention to his application and decided to actually care about Josiah not just as a music clinician for the church, but as a soul that needed nurturing. When he inquired about it, Josiah somehow felt comfortable with sharing the truth.

This is another reason I adored the Blackwells. They had a way of getting through to Josiah, even when he wanted to shut everyone out. Even still, this time seemed different.

Josiah seemed to be in a dark sunken place. As if he was drowning and refused to cry out to anyone for anything.

Oddly enough, his dilemma seemed familiar. We were both angry, we were both sad, we were both hurting, falling apart and broken, yet too proud and unsure of how to receive help while wandering in our dark forest. Paul hit the nail on the head when he said in Romans 7:15, "I don't really understand myself, for I want to do what is right, but I don't do it. Instead, I do what I hate. But if I know that what I am doing is wrong, this shows that I agree that the law is good. So, I am not the one doing wrong, it is sin living in me that does it."

Chapter 12
Looking for Love in All the Wrong Places
– Aliyah

Josiah had been gone now for a little over a month. I felt like I was losing my mind. In the beginning of course I tried to play it cool, like I didn't care that he was gone. I told myself I was fine without him and didn't miss him. Lies, LIES and MORE LIES! I missed the hell out of that man. When I learned that he was staying with Tiffeny, I was speechless. It felt like my stomach fell below my feet! I'd never felt pain like that before in my life. I tried confronting him before he left home to ask him if he was seeing her. At first, he denied it. But all the signs pointed to affair.

When we saw Tiffeny at church, she was nothing but smiles. Her gaze at me was something different though. She looked at me with almost a sly smirk of satisfaction and laughter. I couldn't understand how someone could get such pleasure in taking from someone and hurting people. That is simply not something that I could relate to. What Tiffeny didn't realize though is how I'd saved her from many ass whoopings. When Cammie saw her, she stayed ready to go up side this girl's head, but I brought Cammie back to reality every time by reminding her where we were and who she was. I must say, that was NOT an easy task.

The last time I confronted Josiah about his dealings with Tiffeny and why she was so comfortable calling him all hours of the night, he responded with his request to separate. He said he'd needed some space and had to sort through things to determine if he wanted to stay married. He explained how things just weren't working between us and how he needed a break. That of course didn't sit well with me, but what do you do? I had to let him go. As those days and nights passed, I'm pretty sure I cried every one of them. I tried my best to make sure little Josiah didn't see me. He overheard me once or twice and I made something up like I'd just watched a sad movie. What would really pierce my heart was when he'd come to my room crying every night asking for his daddy and I didn't have an answer for him. I felt bad because I not only felt bad for not being able to bring his daddy back to him, but I felt bad because I felt like it was all my fault that his daddy was gone.

A few weeks after Josiah had left, one of his friends, Cameron, called and started coming by to check on me and little Josiah to make sure we were ok. I thought it was really sweet that he cared enough to even think of us during that time.

He'd heard about everything going on, said he tried reasoning with Josiah, but couldn't get through to him. So, he decided to at least make sure we had someone looking out for us at the house. The communication was harmless, but the phone calls and text messages became regular. Of course, the conversation consisted primarily of me venting about how upset I was about everything going on. By that time, rumors had started to float around about Tiffeny possibly being pregnant with Josiah's child. I'd stopped attending church because I was too ashamed to show my face. At the same time, I was too angry and broken to face Tiffeny or Josiah knowing the rumors had obviously proven to be true.

Instead, Cameron became my outlet. I was surprised he continued to listen to me vent about the nonsense on a daily. Surprisingly, he never really disrespected Josiah by calling him out of his name. Cameron said he was really just trying to be there for me. Cameron was about two years my senior. He had two children. One boy and one girl, who both lived with their mother. Even though he didn't have full custody of his children, he saw them often and made sure he spent time with them and provided for them financially. Cameron's kindness and character traits were attractive. During this season of my life, I wasn't sure how to interpret all the attention from Cameron. It didn't help that he was sexy as hell either. Cameron was about 6', caramel skinned with a fade and beautiful soft curls at the top. He was also a member of the beard game. He wasn't skinny but he was stalky and looked like he could bench press about a good 250. The man was truly one of God's beautiful creations. He was there for me when I was alone. He picked up little Josiah on days that he knew I was having a rough time and would take him to spend time with him and his kids. Essentially, Cameron was a beautiful distraction. A distraction that, because of my broken state, I may have misinterpreted to mean something more just to fill a void that clearly no man could fulfill. I didn't realize that at the time.

It was late Saturday evening. My mom had just left with little Josiah. He was spending the night with his grandma. I had plans to pick him up late Sunday evening in enough time to get ready for the week. Cameron called to check on me, he stated he was in the neighborhood and asked if I wanted him to stop by. When he came over, the man looked and smelled delicious. I swear it was so hard to focus around him, but he always had a way of taking my mind off of my reality and heartbroken state. We went into the den area apparently there was a game on. I ordered pizza and wings. We sat watched the game, laughed and chilled. Before we knew it, it was 11 o'clock in the evening. It had been a minute for me since I'd been shown this much attention so that clearly had to be the reason behind my next set of actions. Before I knew it, I was leaning in ready to kiss Cameron's soft luscious lickable lips. It was odd though because I felt like Cameron may have been moving backwards as I was leaning inward. That however didn't stop me.

I continued to lean in until we heard, "What in the hell is going on in my house? What the..." Cameron and I both jumped up from the couch. My heart felt as if it was going to burst out of my chest. I looked over to see Josiah yelling and rushing toward us.

"JOSIAH! What are you doing here?" I exclaimed.

"What do you mean what am I doing here, Liyah? This is still my house. What in the hell are ya'll doing in here?" He turned to face Cameron who appeared to still be in shock behind everything.

"Oh, it's like that Cameron? Claiming to be my boy but couldn't wait until I wasn't home to start sniffing up and behind my WIFE! Really...It's like that?"

Cameron tried to talk, but Josiah wouldn't even let him finish. He rushed up on him in his face and began pushing him back with his body, "I oughta bust your skull wide open man. Straight to the white meat. I always knew you was a snake," Josiah hissed.

Cameron yelled, "Josiah man calm down! Nothing happened. Nothing was going to happen. I promise you. We were just hanging out. Liyah, tell him."

He looked at me to interject, but Josiah interrupted before I could say a word, "Oh, Liyah ain't gotta tell me nothing! I came in just in time. She was all in your face ready for whatever ya'll normally do in here on a Saturday evening."

"WHAT?" Cameron and I both exclaimed.

"Josiah man you got it all twisted. I promise." Cameron explained. "Listen, I ain't tryna fight you dude. And it's obvious you and Liyah need to square some things away so I'm going to get out of the way and let y'all talk. I apologize if you feel disrespected man. I was really just tryna be here to help out." Cameron turned around and looked at me to finish his last statement, "Nothing more, nothing less!" After that, he turned grabbed his keys and hat and walked out. I felt so small. I hope I hadn't just ruined a relationship because I was being thirsty for some attention. Lord, what was wrong with me!

"You that hard up Liyah, really? You gotta go messin' with my boys? You couldn't find anyone else?" Josiah remarked.

The audacity! That was the first thing that came to my mind. I turned and looked at Josiah like he had four heads, crazy! Because he had to have been kidding me with that comment. "What are you even doing here, Josiah? We haven't seen you in over a month. You finally decide to show up and then try to pitch a fit about what I'm doing while you're over there living with that tramp! A tramp that's supposedly having your baby! You cannot possibly have the audacity to come in here asking crazy questions. Not after you just abandoned us. Me and your son!" I felt myself getting riled up again and ready to fight, so I stopped talking.

"Give me a break Liyah, you're always so over the top. Didn't nobody abandon y'all. I told you I needed a break. I'm here now to see my son. Where is he?" Josiah snarled.

I explained to him that Josiah was with my mom. I figured he'd leave after that, but when he didn't, my patience grew really thin.

"I can't believe you would go behind my back to mess with one my friends Liyah. That's low down!" He accused.

I began to yell once more, "Nobody is messing with your friend, Josiah. Get a grip on your ego. You're always assuming something."

"That's sure as hell what it looked like to me." Josiah snapped back. He was right. I know what it looked like because in the midst of the loneliness, rejection, and darkness of this trial, I'd lost myself for a moment. I misinterpreted the attention and support Cameron was providing me and almost mistook it to mean something else. Something that was only going to cause more confusion, chaos, and brokenness. I truly needed to get a grip. I realized Josiah had experienced the same rejection when he was home. I realized that he also was hurt from my lack of attention and support that should have been provided.

Yet, I was so stuck in my sunken place, that I wouldn't allow myself to be that person for him. I was lost in my own mistakes. What was I doing? What was I thinking!? Even when I was leaning in toward Cameron to kiss him, Cameron was leaning backwards and pulling away from me because he didn't want to muddy the waters. Josiah, finally tired of yelling and throwing things around the house, decided to storm out of the door and leave. I remained still and in shock. I was left in total disbelief of all that had just transpired.

Chapter 13

Words – Aliyah

Josiah had moved out four months and 16 days ago. Does it seem like I was counting down the days? Well, I most definitely was. In the beginning, each night that passed seemed more painful than the last. Even when Cameron called to deflect my attention and to check on little Josiah, I couldn't get my mind off of Josiah. After the incident, Cameron's visits were far less frequent and short in duration. Considering all that had transpired, I recognized cutting that situation off was best for peace.

***

It was nine o'clock pm on a Friday when there was a knock at my door. I'd thought against not opening the door at first because I wasn't having a good day, I was extremely emotional that day and definitely didn't feel up to being bothered. But whoever was at the door was relentless and refused to leave. I'm guessing it was because my car was parked out front, so they knew I was home.

I flung open the door irritated because I wanted whoever it was to stop knocking and go away! I couldn't believe what I was seeing. Absolutely speechless. It was Tiffeny.

She was all smiles of course. I know it wasn't nothing but the Holy Ghost that prevented me from snatching her up by her hair and bashing her face on the side of the house right then and there. She had the nerve to stand there with no words as if she was waiting for me to give her some kind of greeting.

When she continued to stand there smiling and had yet to say a word, I moved to slam the door in her face.

Before I could close it, she yelled, "Hi Aliyah! I'm so sorry to bother you and I hope I didn't interrupt anything."

I stopped before closing it all the way and decided to respond with, "What and why are you at my house?"

Tiffeny continued to smile and responded with, "I'm here to pick up little Josiah for Siah."

My blood began to boil. First of all, did she just call him "Siah"? What the hell is that? Just before I gave in to the flesh and decided to snatch her by her neck, little Josiah ran to the door, and greeted Tiffeny with his small voice.

"Hi Ms. Tiffeny! Where's daddy?" Tiffeny's smile grew wider.

She kneeled down to talk to him, "Hi lil J. I was going to pick you up and take you to your daddy."

I chimed in of course, "Well...she was, but Ms. Tiffeny realized that she had somewhere else to go and shove a few things. She also remembered she had lost her mind and how mommy's house isn't somewhere that she will be visiting anymore. So, tell Ms. Tiffeny bye, bye!"

Josiah looked a little confused, but still smiled and said, "Bye, Ms. Tiffeny! I hope you find your mind. Those are important."

I immediately slammed the door. I told little Josiah to go upstairs and turn up his tv really loud. Something he was never allowed to do. But this time, mommy wanted him to do it just for fun. He laughed and ran upstairs excited to try this experiment.

As he ran up the stairs, I opened the door again and walked outside as Tiffeny was headed to her car.

I calmly told her, "I know you stand in the church and sing all day, but I doubt that you're familiar with the Word. So, let me just share one scripture that you should strongly consider and sincerely take heed to, Proverbs 14:12, 'There is a way that appears to be right, but in the end, it leads to death'."

I crept in closer to her and shared, "You are not welcome here at mine and my husband's home ever in your life and don't you forget it. If you plan on living to see another day, you'd be wise to keep your damn distance."

"Listen little girl, what you fail to realize is the only reason Josiah is with you is because he is mad at me."

I paused for a moment to let that sink in. "Do you still feel special little ugly?" I hissed.

Tiffeny smiled again, "Oh Liyah. . ." she stopped to chuckle.

"Sweetie," she sighed in this condescending tone. "Siah will be by later this week to get the remainder of his things. I understand how it must hurt, but you have to let go of this fantasy that he's ever coming back here. He clearly made his choice and it wasn't you. I mean ...and it makes sense really. You couldn't make up your mind whether or not you even wanted him and didn't show him any respect or support when he was here. Women like you don't deserve a man. You really should just commit yourself solely to Christ because the probability of you finding a man now, at your age and looking like... this..."

She looked me up and down, "The chances are highly unlikely. But Siah's happy now. Really happy, and if you care about him like you claim that you do, you should let him go so that he can be happy, sweetie. So, WE..." She paused to let that sink in.

"Can be happy." She finished.

Before I knew it, I'd run up on her and she broke every acrylic nail on her fingers trying to open the door to jump in her car. I tapped on the window, well more like beat on the window because it cracked.

I shouted, "You selfish, slithering, slimy, sick Bi. . ." I caught myself before I said the word.

"Stay away from my home and my child. When the Lord saves my husband and reveals to him who you really are, you better hope he still has enough mercy in his heart to hold me back to keep me from whooping your entire ass!"

By that time, she'd started up her car and was speeding off, I picked up a rock and threw it. I had real good aim though. The rock landed on her back window and cracked it. My blood was boiling. My hands were shaking and I'm sure my face was fiery red.

I turned to walk back in my home when I noticed a few of my neighbors outside staring at me in disbelief and disgust. There I stood in the middle of my street in my house robe, head wrap, and slippers. I couldn't believe any of this was happening.

I was turning into someone I didn't even recognize. Out here fighting in the streets like I was one of those people on Love and Hip-Hop Gospel Edition. I stood there, breathed in a few breaths to calm my nerves, picked my head up, and walked back into my home with the little dignity I had left.

When I walked through the door, thankful that Josiah was still upstairs watching Paw Patrol with the sound blazing on what sounded like 100, I fell to my knees and wept.

I cried out to my heavenly Father screaming, "Lord, I know I put myself in this situation. I'm not blameless and all I can say is I'm sorry. Forgive me for my broken state, for my attitude, for my wrong. Lord, please get me out of this mess. Please show me what to do."

To say that I really needed God to work a miracle in my life right then, was an understatement.

Chapter 14
The Valley of the Shadow of Death –
Josiah

Folks stayed talking trash. Everybody had something to say about my situation. These are precisely the reasons I did not want to take the position as Young Adult Pastor. I am not the one to be leading any of God's people.

Sometimes, I can't even stand these people. I made a vow that I was no longer living for anyone else. No longer making decisions for anyone else. Regardless of how they felt, what they thought, or what they thought they heard the Lord say, I'm no longer living for other people, I'm living for Josiah Zachariah Williams ONLY.

I sat in the rehearsal hall after rehearsal one day packing up my things getting ready to head out. Tiff walked back in to let me know that she was going to go sit in the car to wait for me because she was tired from a long day at work followed by rehearsal. She was worn out.

I kissed her lips and told her, "Ok baby, I'll be there shortly. Go turn the car on and lay down. I should only be about another ten minutes. . . if that."

As Tiff turned to walk away, I heard someone clearing their throat. I looked up and saw one of the mothers from the church standing with her arms folded, head cocked to the side, and mouth turned so far up that she looked like she had been sucking on an old sour ass lemon.

Tiff of course was unphased by any of it. She rolled her eyes and strolled slowly by the old bitter nosey woman while wearing that same sexy smile that I could always depend on whenever I was feeling down.

I turned back to my equipment to finish packing without even acknowledging the old woman. I think her name was Mother Baxen. Who knows? It wasn't relevant to my life in anyway shape or form. I carried on with my business. Plus, if she didn't have anything to say, I didn't either.

By the time I was done packing my things, I turned around and the rehearsal hall was empty. I turned all of the lights off and exited the church. I joined Tiff in the car to find her knocked out in a deep unbothered slumber. I guess she really was tired.

As expected, I received a call from Dad Blackwell the next day asking me to meet him at the church at two p.m. in his office. He also made sure to inform me that rescheduling was not an option.

When I showed up to the church, he immediately commented on my drinking again. It never failed; Dad Blackwell could always tell when I'd had a drink. I'm not sure how though. I always made sure to cover up with my sunglasses, I'd literally just put a fresh stick of gum in my mouth, and I sprayed myself with my Burberry for men cologne like always. I stayed fresh and smelling good, any time I stepped foot out in the public. Even from a young age, I took pride in being clean. I didn't play those funktified hit or miss washing your tail type of games. Nawww bruh. That wasn't for me.

Anyway, I came prepared to listen and possibly be sat down or even worse, fired. I had another church lined up though. It wasn't paying as much as TBNDC Fellowship, but I had it figured out. If I played multiple services at a few different locations, I could make up for the difference and would still be ok to pay for...everything.

After ten minutes of just staring at me with no words spoken between the two of us, dad finally broke silence and asked, "How far along is she?"

I remained quiet.

He repeated himself, "How far along is she?"

I finally decided to reply to his question with a question, "How far along is who?" I snapped.

"Let's not play these games Josiah. I've seen Tiffeny walking in the church all tired, with that pregnant glow and she's picking up weight. So how far along is she?"

Regardless of how hard I wanted to be. How right or wrong I felt I was, when I talked to Dad Blackwell, he always had a way of pulling out my emotions, tearing down my pride, and reading me like a book. Half the time, I didn't even have to say anything. Dad would just look at me and know something was up.

So, I responded, "5 months."

What's really crazy is that Tiffeny had just told me last week after bible study when I asked her why she seemed to be so tired lately. That's when she finally told me, with all smiles of course, that she was pregnant. So, if I'd just found out about the baby, how did Dad Blackwell know already?

"Ok, and you're sure it's yours?" Dad inquired.

"Yes sir," I choked, but spit it out.

"Does Aliyah know?" He continued speaking while moving

some papers around on his desk and filing them away.

"And, how is she? I haven't seen her in a while. I've tried calling, but she won't answer nor return any of my calls," Dad said sadly.

I sighed heavily and followed with, "I'm sure she does know. She started texting me when the rumors started floating around. Somehow it got out that Tiffeny was pregnant. I didn't confirm or deny when Liyah asked me though."

When dad asked me if I'd seen Little Josiah, is when I unwillingly and uncontrollably felt the tears falling from my eyes. Even with the Versace sunglasses on, he could see the tears streaming down my face. At that point, I made no attempt to catch them, I just let them fall. My reaction alone was enough for my dad to understand where I stood in life and the feelings of failure that haunted me about my family and son. I knew I'd disappointed my dad. I let everyone down.

Honestly, the only thing left realistically for me to do was, die. I couldn't understand for the life of me why God was still allowing me to walk around this earth and even this church. I didn't deserve any of it. Truthfully, I didn't want any of it. My son would later grow up to hate me and now I have this new . . . baby. I just couldn't believe any of this was really happening.

Some nights I tried to drink myself to death. There were days that I actually woke up in ditches passed out in my car, but still. . . I woke up. Why? What was the Lord waiting on to take me out of here?

Liyah made several attempts to call me and ask about me, but why? She'd proven when I was home that she didn't want me or need me. My biggest disappointment with myself is that I allowed all of this to pull me away from my son, little Josiah. He didn't deserve any of this. But honestly, I was so far gone, I couldn't see any way back.

I wasn't sure how to fix things with my son, with the church, with Dad Blackwell, Liyah, or Tiff. I honestly couldn't even tell you what Tiff saw in me, other than her supporting me and my ability to sing and play.

Perhaps she just wanted someone that accepted her for who she was. She didn't care who it was or whose I was. We made a dynamic team in the musical aspect. Outside of that, I wasn't quite sure what we had to offer one another. I was so run down, but Tiff appeared to still love me. I guess I should have been grateful to have that much.

I was certain of one thing though, there was no way of fixing any of this. I was definitely too far gone in life for redemption. My plan was to just ride things out this way until I breathed my last breath. It was evident that happiness was no longer in the cards for me. Not after all that I had messed up.

I sat face-to-face with my spiritual dad awaiting final word concerning my employment status. After a brief silence that seemed to last a lifetime, he attempted to say something, but I interrupted him with, "For the wages of sin is death dad. . .Romans 6:23."

I hoped that with this reminder, dad would just leave me alone and let me die. He looked at me with empathetic eyes and said, "Son, all wrongdoing is sin, and there is sin that does not lead to death", 1 John 5:17. "There is no peace, says my God, for the wicked." I quoted Isaiah 57:21 in a defeated and defiant tone urging him to backdown. "There is no peace, says my God."

Dad continued with a smirk on his face, "Ok, if we confess our sins, God is faithful and just to forgive us our sins and to cleanse us from all unrighteousness." I stood up at this point.

"Oh, what a miserable person I am! Who will free me from

this life that is dominated by sin and death?" I spoke firmly. Romans 7:24.

Dad slammed his fist against his desk and stood while shouting, "Thank God! The answer is Jesus Christ our Lord! So now there is no condemnation for those who belong to Christ Jesus. And because you belong to Him, the power of the life-giving Spirit has freed you from the power of sin that leads to death! Get up and reclaim your life boy! Stop taking up residency in Lodebar, the land of exile, shame and bondage. All of us at one point in time have operated outside of God's grace and love. I don't care where you came from, what mistakes you've made, who wasn't there for you like you thought they should have been growing up! Those are all excuses you've used to sit and stew in your sin! You know better now, so you do better! And you better wake up because it's never too late to get things right with God. Stop letting the enemy fool you about that woman, Josiah. It's witchcraft and trickery. She is your Delilah son. The whole relationship is draining you of all your power and strength. You're drunk, depressed, drowning and appearing as though you are defeated. How is this building you up? Open your eyes Josiah! The way that situation was formed was totally outside of the will of God and it will NEVER be blessed!"

I had to stop him before he busted a blood vessel from being so emotionally riled up.

"I hear you dad and I know I disappointed you!"

"It's not about you disappointing me boy," he lashed back.

"YES, IT IS!" I shouted. I paused, took a breath and began trying to explain, "I really did believe I could be better a long time ago. And Why the Lord chose me, I honestly couldn't tell you. In the beginning, I was glad He did."

I could barely get the words out clearly because of the tears and sorrow of weeping. I choked at every sound I made.

"But now, not so much. Don't get me wrong. I love my ministry. It's a blessing to be able to not only do what I love, but I also get paid to do it all day every day. I'm not like you Dad! This ain't easy for me. I'm a complete stranger to this lifestyle and the expectations of God's people are impossible! It's like I can never please anyone. Not the church, not my friends…not even my family! I guess that's why Proverbs 29:25 says, 'The fear of human opinion disables us...' And that part right there, is exactly what crippled me."

Sadly, I wasn't just what others thought about me, but I felt

I wasn't worthy of anything. I wasn't what I thought could have been, but I tried! I'm just so angry, so overwhelmed, and sick of all the Got damn rejection. I'm fed up with chasing after people that don't want me and reject me as if I'm nothing and don't matter. All of these responsibilities on me as a husband and a father and then the church... heck, LIFE! Then people expect me to be perfect.

At this point I could feel that I was spitting because I was over enunciating each word I spoke at full volume at the top of my vocal ability. Still, that didn't matter, I needed to be heard. If dad wanted to read me for my mistakes, then he needed to make sure he had all the damn facts!

"People are constantly watching you and expecting you to have all the right answers ALL the time. And the bottom line is . . . I DON'T! There's a lot that I'm still learning. Once you pronounce salvation or obtain a title in the church, it's a wrap. You're expected to be Jesus from then on out. And now..." I paused, collapsed in my seat and began to sob like a baby, "I've proven them right! I was a failure, an adulterer, an alcoholic like my biological father. So, I'm ready for Karma to come and kick my ass."

Dad walked over and laid his hands on my shoulders. His tone was softer than it was during our heated encounter earlier, "You're flawed son."

I chuckled a condescending "that's obvious" chuckle from the statement he'd just made.

"That's an understatement, sir."

Dad continued, "In all that you've been through son, you can't forget all that you've learned about who God is. Now is the time to remember that the God we serve uses flawed people to reach His people in this flawed world. Who better to understand them? Not only that, but when you really think about things, aren't imperfect people all God really has? His word doesn't lie. We all have sinned and come short of His glory. So, since we all sin and there isn't one that we can call blameless, we've got to learn how to exercise grace and mercy as God does for us. Perhaps you've forgotten what that looks like because I'm not sure that grace or mercy was something you showed Liyah when she was down and out."

Although it stung and irritated me to hear him say that, I knew he was telling the truth, the whole truth and nothing but the truth.

"Josiah, I need you to really listen to me son. Life is full of tests. But, it's about lessons. Deuteronomy 8 says, 'remember how the Lord your God led you all the way in the desert these forty years, to humble you and to test you in order to know what was in your heart, whether or not you would keep his commands.' I'm not going to lie to you son, you messed up."

He paused to look at me then continued, "Son, you messed up REAL bad.

. . But, what did you learn? We ALL go through things in life, the point of it all surrounds what you take away from life's encounters. That's how you not only grow, but how you become able to help others who stumble upon the same journeys of life."

I sat and listened, waiting for him to finish as I continued trying to regain my composure.

"Now, unfortunately, there are some people who struggle secretly and it's not visible for many to see so to the naked eye, those people's lives are seemingly perfect, but you and I both know that it's not the truth because of what the word of God says. No one is perfect."

I looked at him and responded with, "Yeah, I wasn't that fortunate. My business is all over the place."

Dad continued, "That's when you know you're chosen. Your test and trials were exposed for a great purpose. Josiah, understand that there is a reason that God wanted so many people to witness your journey. God even allowed this pregnancy to continue and people to see it for a reason. I can't tell you what it is because I don't know. But, there was a purpose to people seeing your successes when you were up and also having the opportunity to witness your failures when you are down. You're an influential Minister Josiah Zachariah, it's time for you to get up, repent and reclaim your life. You can recover from this. God can still get the Glory if you only allow Him. It's out there, they've seen your test, now allow them to witness your turnaround!"

What dad was saying was getting to me, but I just couldn't see how I could change now. I literally felt like there was no way of turning back for me. Not now. I had to see this thing through.

"Dad, with all due respect, I hear you, but I have to sort through this on my own. There really isn't anyone that can tell me anything. I'm over being judged and condemned for my mistakes," I explained.

He sat down, took a deep breath in and finally exhaled.

"I believe there's a little bit of what you know about the Lord and who He's called you to be left inside of you. I know it seems dark right now, but don't let the darkness fool you. God is still present, and He is still God. Once you release this pain, this anger, this bitterness and brokenness, allow forgiveness to set in, you will be able to witness the turnaround of this test. Surrender to Him in all of His love, forgiveness, grace and goodness. That part, is going to be entirely up to you, son. Your choice."

"How do you know I haven't chosen God or that I'm not still praying and talking to God?"

"Because you showed up here drunk and broken. Just like you do in every service. That's not the behavior of someone who is walking in the forgiveness and love that God has provided. That's the behavior of someone who is walking in unhappiness, self-condemnation and defeat."

Dad's reply definitely had me stuck and speechless.

He continued, "Once you get tired, truly sick and tired of being down and living in this place that you know you don't belong, with people who you don't belong with, you'll open your heart again to the Lord and allow Him to restore you."

"Are we done here?" I questioned.

Dad paused for a brief moment then replied, "We are, you're

free to go."

As I got up to walk out, he called to me, "Oh, Josiah!" I turned to hear what he had left to say.

"Effective immediately, you are reassigned from Minister of Music. I'll allow you to keep your same salary, but you will be assigned as one of the night security officers monitoring the campus."

If looks could kill, I most definitely would have been entirely responsible for the death of my dad that day. With no words, I took my exit, but not before slamming the door to his office.

I needed to contact the other churches with openings ASAP.

Chapter 15
The Pruning Process – Aliyah

Two weeks had passed, and I hadn't been to work, I hadn't left the house, nor was I answering the phone, and I damn sure wasn't welcoming any visitors. little Josiah went to stay at my moms, I didn't want him to see me in this state; broke down, defeated, sad, miserable, heartbroken, low and funky. No; I mean literally funky. I hadn't showered in days. My hair was matted because I hadn't touched it, and I honestly believed I now had 10 new cavities because I hadn't brushed my teeth either. It was absolutely disgusting. I was disgusted with myself inside and out.

I cried, prayed, cried, and prayed, but it all seemed pointless because my lifestyle showed that I clearly had no expectation of God to do anything that I was requesting of Him. I'd given up hope on receiving anything including healing for myself.

My phone had been ringing off the hook that day, but I continued to ignore it as always. I checked the caller ID to make sure it wasn't my mom calling about Josiah. It showed the church's number. I definitely wasn't answering that.

Who could possibly be calling me from there? I sat down to turn on another episode of Grey's Anatomy when I heard my doorbell and a knock at the door.

Having a flashback of the last time I had an unexpected visitor; I went to the door prepared. I grabbed my baseball bat.

I yelled, "Who is it!"

A soft silky voice replied on the other side of the door, "Liyah baby, it's me First Lady. Can I come in, please?"

I sat there for a couple of minutes unsure of what I wanted to do next. My home nor I were in a condition that was suitable for visitors. I guess I stayed quiet too long. All of a sudden, I heard the door opening.

In shock and somewhat offended, I asked, "How'd you get in here?" She replied with, "I asked Josiah for his key."

I think she waited to see if I was going to push back and request that she leave. I didn't. Despite how I felt, it was still a bit heartwarming to see my beautiful First Lady Blackwell. I missed her and my entire church family. I just couldn't muster the strength to show my face at the church after everything that happened. I was completely humiliated by it all.

First Lady Blackwell walked through the hall and entered the living room where I had cups, plates, trash, clothes, blankets and pillows. As I said before, if I hadn't taken the time to clean myself, you can imagine what my house was looking like. I suggested that she find a seat. She moved one of my blankets to the side and scooted a plate with empty scraps of fried chicken on it out of the way.

I finally broke silence and mumbled with my head hung low, "Excuse the mess. I just haven't gotten around to cleaning up. Of course, I wasn't expecting visitors either, but still. I'm sorry about the mess."

Lady Blackwell responded with this look of love, compassion, and sincere heart ache in her eyes, "Liyah, Baby. I know it hurts, and honestly, none of it makes sense right now..."

I cut her off with, "That's pretty close to explaining it, but words can't even express the pain, sadness, hurt, and anger that I feel right now. I mean, I get it. I wasn't the best wife; I could have done some things better. I hate that I was broken. I feel like I broke my husband Lady Blackwell. I broke my husband and my marriage. How do I live with myself after this? I have to look little Josiah in the eyes and find ways to comfort him when he cries to me at night begging for me to get his daddy to come home. In my heart, I know he's absent because I hurt him. How do I live with that shame and guilt?"

First Lady Blackwell only shook her head in sadness. She looked at me and asked, "What happened? Why do you think you weren't the best wife?"

I went on to explain to her how I'd let baggage from my past carry into my marriage. I never talked about this with anyone before, but I shared with her the story of me being sexually molested by my mom's friend's daughter at the age of eight. Of course, I'd heard people talk about sexual molestation, but I wasn't sure if my situation fell under that category because she wasn't a grown up. She was a teenager. She was still a kid herself.

I remember growing up, always wondering if I, myself, was a lesbian. I blocked out the memories of the trauma and as a result grew up hating myself, my body, and who I was because of everything that I went through. I was able to function and live through it, but never fully healed.

When I got married, and had little Josiah, it was like everything about me came unglued. I was unstable in so many ways and the brokenness came rushing back like a flood into my life negatively impacting my husband and my child.

First Lady Blackwell sat quietly listening to it all. I glanced at her while revealing so many deep dark personal secrets about myself. I watched for her facial expression to change and wondered if she was grossed out by my experiences and disappointed by my treatment toward her son, Josiah.

I cried when trying to get her to understand how I didn't want any of this to happen. I wished terribly that I could fix it.

After listening to me talk for what seemed like forever, she finally chimed in, "You know, life has a way of always giving us what we need. God designed things that way. Knowing all that you went through and all that you would do, your Heavenly Father still allowed you to get married. God knew you would make these very mistakes and end up where you are."

I cut her off, "Why would he allow me to make such a huge mess of things?"

She continued, "Just like He knew where you were in life and the hurt you harbored inside, He knew how broken your husband was as well. God gives us free will to choose of course. The two of you chose each other in your broken states. What came about during these tests and trials was revelation. God allowed all of the brokenness, hurt, and insecurities to be revealed. Not just in you baby girl, but in your husband as well. Look at the young girl he's chosen right now. She's younger than he is and obviously broken to want and have pursued a married man. Josiah may not realize it yet, but he's following a pattern of choosing broken women with insecurities because it's how he feels. You and I both know my son's history and how he grew up. He experienced constant rejection which resulted in him making it a habit to doubt his worthiness. Now, he's extremely humiliated by the mistakes he's made in front of the people he wanted to prove that he could be someone better. Now, he feels obligated to make the mess that he made work. Pride and hurt is a rough combination, and it has a strong hold on that boy because he knows he's wrong. But he has publicly humiliated himself and has no clue how to come back into God's grace. He's forgotten how simple that is."

First Lady continued as I wept, "The Lord is trying to show the both of you what areas you need to work on in order to receive total healing. Total healing as individuals in order to come together. You're going to need that total healing to receive a turnaround in your own life. All of these lessons in life are fermenting you for what's next. That's why it's so important to be careful not to get stuck in this place of pain, baby girl. Accept all of these painful processes as lessons! You've got to declare ruling over your feelings and work through this process to forgive and heal. You'll need to start with forgiving yourself of course. When you started off explaining everything, you stated how all of this was your fault. Although you played your part, don't take ownership of this entire catastrophe Aliyah. Josiah deserves some credit as well. Next, you'll have to work on forgiving Josiah and Tiffeny and whoever else hurt you in your past. I want to encourage you to speak with a counselor to help you sort through some of these things. It can be a lot, but YOU CAN get through this. I know right now it probably sounds like I just cursed you with that request to forgive, but trust me, it's necessary. It's necessary for complete and total healing. That's what we're striving for."

I picked my face up, wiped my tears, and responded, "Yes ma'am."

"And Liyah..." First Lady Blackwell called out to me, "Get up and clean yourself up baby. Go brush your teeth, wash your face, take a shower, and shine like the beautiful diamond that you are! Don't ever let anyone take that from you. That part of you is what God put in you. It's how He created you. So regardless of what Tiffeny, Josiah, or the lost soul who tried to rob you of your childhood and dignity when you were younger, regardless of what they dish out, you remember who you are in Christ. Even with my son Josiah. It's nice to have him in your life as your 'better half' should he choose to do that. It is beautiful to have him a part, but it's not necessary! Josiah is not your God. The Lord gifted you to be great with Him and Him alone. Don't you ever lose sight of that either."

Chapter 16
Don't Wait till Midnight – Josiah

I was out at a bar that night, one that was pretty far removed from the city because I didn't want people from the church in my business or passing judgement. My phone was blowing up, I was receiving back to back phone calls from Liyah. She was adamant and persistent with requesting to talk to me. I could tell that by the many text messages she was sending to my phone. I tried to ignore her, but the last message she sent pissed me off. It read that she was on her way to Tiffeny's house.

So, I picked up the phone to call her. I stepped out. I needed to take the call outside to avoid making a scene inside the bar. I had to run and jump in my car because it was raining pretty bad. As soon as she answered, I screamed at Liyah asking what the heck she was doing and to not even bother going over to Tiffeny's house because I wasn't there. I swear sometimes Liyah did too much. That was just flat out messy.

She inquired as to where I was, and I didn't respond. She said she was driving and demanded to know where I was. She sounded frantic. Something in me started to worry a little so I asked where little Josiah was.

Liyah continued screaming about how she only wanted to talk to me to clear the air. She finally interjected that little Josiah was with her mom.

She continued to say, "I need to talk to you now, Josiah! Please just tell me where you are. It's important. I owe you an apology."

She began crying hysterically. I tried several times asking her to calm down. I could hear the rain pouring down on her end of the phone as well. There was even thunder and lightning. I fussed at her to go back to the house and that I would talk to her later, now just wasn't a good time. Liyah insisted that it had to be tonight.

Finally, I asked her to calm down and pull over because the weather was crazy. When I asked where she was, I heard a loud horn honking in the background and Liyah began screaming. I heard tires screeching and finally a large "BOOM!"

I screamed, "Liyah!! Aliyah answer me, please!!"

All I could hear on the other end of the phone was the sound of a constant horn blowing. I screamed Liyah's name a few more times only to receive no response. My heart pounded and my head began to spin.

I finally remembered that I had Apple's *Find My Phone* app downloaded and Liyah's phone was still connected to mine so I pinged her location. I grabbed a cup of coffee and it was nothing but the grace of God that allowed me to sober up that quick. I followed the directions using the find my phone app only to pullup to the location of the accident to see the paramedics hauling Aliyah away on a stretcher.

My heart fell below my knees. I began screaming her name. The police grabbed me and made several attempts to calm me down. I didn't remember doing this, but apparently, I called Aliyah's mom and explained what happened.

After I explained to the police and paramedics that I was Liyah's husband, they told me which hospital they were taking her to. When I asked to ride, they refused because they said they couldn't work with me in the way. They couldn't work?? That meant she wasn't conscious. I was damn sure panicking now. I pulled up to Liyah's car appearing to be completely wrapped around a light pole with a semi-truck smashed into the back of her 2017 Altima. It was a miracle that Liyah even made it out of the car.

When I got to the hospital, Liyah's mom was there with little Josiah because she said she didn't have anyone else to leave him with. I was completely losing my mind. I was screaming at the nurses working triage demanding for someone to tell me where my wife was! They reassured me the paramedics had already brought her in and that Liyah was back in surgery. They explained that one of the doctors would be out soon. After two and a half hours, that seemed like an eternity, one of the surgeons came out and told us that Liyah was in a coma.

Upon hearing this news, her mom immediately broke down and started crying. I grabbed a hold of her trying to keep her from hitting the ground. I told the doctor to continue. I needed to know what this meant. The surgeon explained that Liyah pulling through this was going to be deemed a definite miracle because she had actually flown through the windshield.

The surgeon explained that in itself was an odd miracle because had she stayed in the car, and the way it was demolished, there's no way that she would have survived. So, her being thrown out of the car was a blessing. At this point, there was a lot of swelling on her brain, her arm was broken, and of course quite a bit of cuts and bruises. The surgeon encouraged us to stay prayerful and give it time.

From what the police and doctors explained, it appeared that Liyah had hydroplaned, lost control of her car, spun out of control, crossed lanes, and hit a light pole, while also throwing a semi off course and the truck loss control as well.

Thankfully, the truck driver was ok and no one else was injured. I glanced over at my son, little Josiah, who was over in one of the chairs sleeping peacefully unaware of what was happening. That's definitely how I wanted it. My pants pocket was vibrating. I moved to answer the phone and it was Tiffeny asking if I was ok and wondering where I was in such bad weather. I shared with her that there'd been an accident and that I was at the hospital with Liyah. Tiffeny sighed. She asked if I needed her to come as a support for me or if I needed her to come get little Josiah.

I immediately snapped back, "No, just stay home. It's too dangerous out here for you to be driving."

By that time, Liyah's friends Cammie and Michele had already shown up to the hospital. I knew if Tiffeny came up there, it would be a misunderstanding in the waiting room of that hospital. By the time I got off of the phone Dad and First Lady Blackwell, Liyah's brother, and so many others had already made their way up to the hospital and were praying in the waiting area. I was an emotional mess. I was simply waiting for the doctors to give me the all clear to go in the room to see her.

After an hour passed, Cammie and Michele agreed to take little Josiah back home to sleep in his bed. I told them I'd call as soon as I had an update. There wasn't a dry eye in that waiting area. I demanded that no one stop praying.

I was so angry at myself. She was out looking for me! If only I'd been home or at the church or somewhere that she could come to easily to find me, none of this would have happened. By the time I finished fussing at myself internally, the surgeon walked up and told me that I could now go back to see her. Only two to three people were allowed at a time. And everyone in there knew I was automatically going to be considered one of the three, unless they were ready to fight me for my spot. I wasn't going anywhere. Liyah's mom, Dad Blackwell, and I walked back to her room. As we entered and saw her head bandaged, her face all cut up, and tubes connected to her, I fell to the ground. Dad Blackwell did everything in his power to lift me up, but I couldn't stop sobbing like a baby. I couldn't stand seeing Liyah like this.

She had to wake up for little Josiah, for her mom, for...me! As Dad Blackwell began to pray, I sobbed loudly, held her hand and prayed to the Lord, who I hadn't talked to in long while. I begged God to bring her back to me. I wasn't sure if the Lord would hear me after all the wrong I'd done, but I was definitely going to try to get this prayer through for Liyah.

She didn't deserve this. I even begged the Lord to allow us to trade places. None of this was right and it didn't seem fair. God was up to something and all I knew is that I really needed a miracle and for my wife to open her eyes. I stayed at the hospital day in and day out for weeks. Against my advisement, Tiffeny had made her way up to the hospital one day. She said it was because she hadn't seen me, and I was spending too much time up there. That day Liyah's mom was there with little Josiah. Tiffeny saw him and walked over to him. She hugged him and asked if he was ok. My mother-in-law wasn't enthused by any of this of course. Tiffeny then asked little Josiah if he wanted to go with her while everyone else stayed to check on mommy.

Of course, my son lost it. He began hollering that he wanted his mommy! He wanted mommy right now! It shocked Tiffeny because she clearly had no clue that he would respond that way. I rushed to little Josiah and calmed him down. Tiffeny went to rub my face and arm then asked if I needed anything. I pushed her hand off of me and explained I only needed her to go home. Her presence was not helping anything or anyone. Tiffeny looked at me in extreme shock, irritation, and disgust. She snatched her purse off of the chair. She began walking off, but not before turning around to ask, "What time will you be home Siah?" As I held my still sobbing son, I turned away, rolled my eyes, and requested that she just go. I sat with Liyah the entire day. Still no signs of her waking up anytime soon.

I was definitely discouraged and scared out of my mind. It was then, I felt Liyah's middle finger twitch. I jumped up and called for the doctor. By the time the doctor walked in, Liyah was shaking her head and opening her eyes. You would think this would have been a happy moment for me, but I teared up. Would she remember it was my fault that she crashed? If she did, would she ever forgive me? Lord, did I deserve forgiveness for all that I'd done to my family? If it were left up to me, absolutely not! I deserved nothing from them, and I definitely didn't deserve anything from the Lord.

Chapter 17

Faith & Forgiveness, It Takes Two – Josiah

It had been several weeks since the accident. Liyah was home, healed, and doing well. It's like the surgeon said, Aliyah Ariyanna was definitely a walking miracle. Truth be told; she's always been one if you ask me.

Since then, I'd been by often to spend time with little Josiah, but even that never felt like enough. When I entered the house, it smelled wonderful as it always did, like fresh linen and lavender.

Liyah did take good care to keep the house together even while I was gone. If something needed to be fixed, she'd fix it, or find someone else to fix it. All this while working, taking primary care of little Josiah, and dealing with the crap I was giving her. She was so strong, even when I wasn't. I walked to the living room, but I didn't see Liyah. I moved into the kitchen, still no Liyah. Before panicking, I then walked upstairs into our...well her bedroom and found Liyah on her knees praying and crying out to God. I wasn't trying to eavesdrop by listening in, but I didn't want to interrupt either.

In fact, my mind was blown when I heard what Liyah began praying about. This woman was actually interceding for me. After all I'd done, said, and shown her. After the car crash and all the disappointment I'd caused her and Josiah, I couldn't believe that she would still want to pray for me? That shocked the hell out of me.

I heard her saying, "Lord, BLESS my husband. Save his soul, touch his mind, and heal his hurt. Father forgive us for the pain we've caused one another. Forgive us for the disappointment, devastation, and discord we've sown. Renew a right spirit in us. Lord open the eyes of Josiah's heart. Bring him back to you, Oh God! Deliver him, set him free from this captivity stemmed from feelings of defeat. Help him to see that it is not the end for him! But, only the beginning of a new more intimate and more powerful connection with you..."

I stood quietly allowing her to finish without interruption. She went into asking God to forgive her for the anger, bitterness and hardness in her heart. She then transitioned into praying for little Josiah. I waited until it seemed like she was ready to conclude her conversation with the Lord and I noticeably cleared my throat out loud. It startled her a bit because she jumped while kneeling in her praying position. Liyah wiped her tears that rolled down her cheeks.

She stood facing me and asked in a soft soothing tone, "Hey Josiah, what are you doing here? I didn't hear you come in."

Liyah still had a small scar above her eye from the accident, but I swear, as hurt as I was by her and angry from the whole situation, Liyah was still the most beautiful woman in the world to me. There were times I hated looking at her because it would awaken things in me that I wanted to keep buried and hidden deep down inside.

She made me face reality and my truths. Yet those truths and that reality was what forced me to face the pain. Man, even after everything, I still felt like this woman was so much to me.

I responded, "I used my key."

Liyah chuckled, "Oh, you got it back from Mom Blackwell?" I laughed almost forgetting that mom did harass me for that key just to get to Liyah a while back.

"Yeah, she returned it. Listen, I didn't mean to interrupt you. I just thought I'd stop by to see little Josiah and ummm...to check on you. How are you? You look great." I expressed nervously.

She responded with, "I am well. Little Josiah should be in his room playing. He just had a snack and wanted to go play with his slime set. I pray it's not all over the floor or furniture. I swear I hate that stuff." We both chuckled.

"Yeah, me too, but he loves it," I responded.

"I was going to take little Josiah out to lunch. . ."

Liyah anxiously responded, "Absolutely! He'd love that. He's already dressed. I'll grab his shoes and a small sweater since it's a little breezy out." She rushed past me to go gather his items.

I honestly can't say what made me go there, but I said, "Would you like to go? I'd like it if you joined us."

I swallowed deep and waited for what seemed like forever for her to respond.

"Are you sure? I don't want to intrude...I mean if you don't mind...I wouldn't mind going," Liyah fumbled her response.

I followed back with, "Great! It's settled. How about we go to BJ's Restaurant? You know it's little Josiah's favorite."

Liyah smiled softly and said, "I'll go get ready."

About an hour had passed. Me, Liyah and little Josiah were

sitting at the table talking over lunch and discussing everything. little Josiah was so excited to be with both of us and it warmed my heart to hear and see how happy he was.

I have to be honest though, it felt weird. I didn't feel worthy to be around them in that aspect. I'd done so much damage that it almost didn't seem right to even be in their presence.

As we sat there laughing and playing "I spy" games, this guy walks over to our table. I looked at Aliyah confused. For a moment, I wondered if this was maybe some dude she'd been messing around with and he decided to walk over to our table and start some mess while my son was there.

If there was one thing I didn't tolerate AT ALL, it was having drama go down in front of my child. I wasn't about that life. I was ready to smash dude's face in if he even thought about tripping in front of my son.

He began with, "Good afternoon. I'm so sorry to bother you."

We all remained quiet except Josiah, he chimed in with, "HI! I'm Josiah!"

The stranger smiled and spoke to little Josiah then returned his eyes to me and continued with, "Is this your family man?"

I responded with, "Yes" while keeping my eyes on this dude watching and waiting for his next move.

"Well I know I don't know you all, but I had to just come over and remind you that you're blessed! Your family is absolutely beautiful!! God has truly blessed you with what you have right here."

He then looked at Liyah and back at me and requested that we take care of each other. Although I was a bit taken aback, I still responded with a thank you and slight smile. Just as quickly as he'd walked up, he turned and walked away.

Maybe five minutes later, the waitress walked up to our table and asked Liyah and I if we needed anything else. She smiled and explained that our bill had been paid for including the tip by the gentleman that had just left. little Josiah was busy coloring. I looked up at Liyah and without warning, tears began to fall from my eyes.

Liyah rushed in to begin wiping the tears as the fell from my face. I couldn't understand the grace I was experiencing. Why the mercy for me? If only this guy knew what we were going through. If he only knew all that I had done, would he still have demonstrated such a kind gesture? I was so overwhelmed with emotion at that moment, I wasn't sure what to say or do.

I looked up at Liyah as she gazed in my eyes and said, "God's faithful and just to forgive us. I'm sorry for hurting you Josiah. I realize I wasn't where I should have been emotionally and mentally or spiritually when we married. For that, I owe you an apology for allowing my brokenness to break your heart and spirit. I can only pray that one day you will forgive me for all the pain I've caused and inflicted on this family."

I sat still unable to stop the tears from running down my face.

I finally looked at Liyah, "There's been too much damage and we simply can't go back..."

Liyah interrupted me, "I don't want to go back, Josiah. Only forward. My past isn't pleasant. There's nothing there I want to revisit. It gave me what I needed to grow closer to the Lord and heal. Nothing about it was a mistake.

Although painful, it was all necessary. Including you."

It was so difficult because when I was around Liyah, every time I looked at her, I was reminded of my pain, distrust, fear, and failure. Yet, I wanted so badly to hand her my heart again, but how? I also knew that I couldn't bear to lose her.

The night of the accident, I came so close, and the feeling that I felt knowing that she might not wake up, made me feel like my heart was literally going to stop beating.

I replied, "Liyah, I've made such a mess of things, I have no clue how to even begin to make my way back from any of this. I lost my position and respect at the church. I walked away from you and Josiah. . . I was so hurt. I guess I have some healing as well to do. Then, I bought Tiffeny into this mess. I involved her in a web of brokenness, lies, and confusion. Now she's pregnant about to have this baby. I feel like I owe her something, but honestly I don't have much of anything that I can give her."

Liyah replied, "Give her respect as the mother of your child, give her support with this baby, and most importantly, give her over to God. The Lord knows how to take care of the rest."

I looked at Liyah and exposed to her how during the time I wasn't able to see little Josiah it was because I was locked up in jail over several DUIs, unpaid parking tickets, and resisting arrest. Dad Blackwell bailed me out a few times, but this last time, he let me sit in there until the judge made a decision to allow me 30 days house arrest.

Dad Blackwell decided to stop helping me so that I could learn. I truly felt like I'd hit rock bottom. I couldn't even fathom or imagine what it would look like to go any lower. It's crazy though, I'd always said I was going to be better than my alcoholic father who left me, my mom, and sister to go be with another woman. I vowed to do better, love better, live better, and always be there for my son. Now, I'm living a life completely opposite of what I vowed to do. That's the failure that I struggle the most with overcoming. I was a full-on hypocrite.

Liyah and I packed up all of the left overs on the table and headed out. I dropped them off and decided to go to the church. Although I was no longer in my position at TBNDC Fellowship, I went in on occasion to use the keyboard.

I must say, for a moment, I barely wanted to play. All the music started to feel the same and it didn't move me. Some days I enjoyed sitting or driving in silence because I didn't want to hear any music.

Today, I wanted to sit in my element, on that keyboard, and play and sing until I felt my release. As I sat and played the keys, I wondered how I was able to allow things to get so bad and so far gone that I literally couldn't see my way back. I fell and fell hard.

Just then, I recalled a conversation Dad Blackwell had with me when he was encouraging me to go back to school. He asked me why I hadn't finished school, then followed that question with another.

"Where do you see yourself in 10 years?"

I had no answer. All I knew is I wanted to play and produce my music.

Dad Blackwell looked at me and said, "Son, that's a wonderful aspiration and it fits you. What steps do you have planned to accomplish this goal?"

I of course remained silent after that question. This man always had a way of making things so deep when I felt like it didn't need to be. He continued with explaining to me how I can sit and dream, or I can actually do something.

Most people choose only to dream because 'doing' takes too much work. Yet, when you think about it, anything worth having will take a lot of work. Luke 12:48 says, "From everyone who has been given much, much will be demanded; and from the one who has been entrusted with much, much more will be asked."

Dad Blackwell explained how it's so easy to sit and do nothing or even to quit. All you have to do is let go and fall.

It takes no real effort at all, but in the end, you're left with nothing as well. He encouraged me to be careful anytime I felt lead to quit.

He said, "Son, to truly have something whether it be wealth, health, success in music or ministry, and even a family, it's going to take work. It's going to take humility, sacrifice, compromise, and commitment."

Remembering these words while sitting at the organ in the sanctuary playing and singing the gospel took me into a place of repentance that I wasn't expecting. I was tired of running, tired of fighting back and quite frankly, I was tired of falling. I'd decided to give God's way a try.

I immediately began to pray, "Heavenly Father, I'm so sorry for all of my sins for all of my wrong Lord. I've hurt people, I've lied and I've cheated. Father please forgive me; I want to be saved. I know your word is true. I know your way is life and I choose life today. I want to live for you. God, show me my way back. Back to your will and purpose for my life."

As I prayed, I realized I had stopped playing and actually made my way down on the floor of the altar. I wept like a baby. If my boys knew how many tears I shed during this season of my life, they'd for sure clown me and call me a "simp", but I couldn't control the tugging at my heart.

The reality finally set in. I lost my wife, the woman I was so madly in love with, that I stopped at nothing in the beginning to make her mine. My son! My first-born son, who when he looked at me, my whole world felt as if it would stop moving just for him. My home! We purchased that home together and now I'm held up in this apartment with, oh my God...what was I doing?

I can't even last longer than eight hours without needing a drink to numb the pain and distract me from my reality. I was tired of having suicidal thoughts. I knew God's word and I prayed that the Lord still had his hand on me.

As soon as that thought crossed my mind, I felt a hand on my shoulder. It was Dad Blackwell. He was crying and began praying out loud with me. Praying for my healing, my total salvation and complete surrender, and turnaround in God. He embraced me while continuing to pray and encouraging me to continue fighting. Continue running back to the Lord and to trust Him with complete surrender because the Lord could do anything but fail.

He told me that God never left my side and that He was going to use this mess up for my move up. Dad Blackwell also shared that God understood why I was confused. He knew that I responded to Aliyah the way that I did based off of what I was familiar with and it was the only way I knew how to be. Yet God's grace is sufficient.

It wasn't too late to return my heart to God and allow him to heal it.

Regardless of what people think or who walked away during my time of struggle, God has new people for my next season, I only needed to surrender to God's will for my life. I said, "YES! Yes, to His will and to His way. I will trust Him and obey!" I sat there at the alter with God for at least an hour finding my way back home.

Chapter 18
The Turn-Around – Josiah

By the time Tiffeny delivered her baby, I was already moved out and was in my own apartment. I did go to the hospital to see our new baby boy. He favored me, but he looked more like his mom. Tiffeny of course didn't take the decision of me moving out very well. In fact, she cursed me out and called me stupid for allowing someone of her caliber to get away. I remained close by and continued providing what financial support I could for the baby.

I even went down to the child support office and put myself on child support. I wanted to make sure there were no misunderstandings in the near future about what support I was providing or what was expected of me. She resisted a bit, but eventually stopped fighting me.

Some days she even dropped our son off to my apartment and would leave him there for days at a time. I wasn't sure what that was about, but it was my son, and I didn't deny him.

As humiliating as it was, I didn't hide him. Anyone who saw me out would see me with both of my boys. little Josiah was too young to understand, but he was enjoying being a big brother.

Things were actually beginning to turn around. I'd stopped drinking and was attending my AA classes regularly. I began studying my Word more and never felt closer to the Lord before in my life. It felt good.

Liyah and I were talking often, we even went on a few dates. It was actually fun. We were learning about each other all over again and providing one another with a clean slate. Just like before, I loved everything about her but now, it felt deeper.

On our third or fourth date, Liyah and I went to dinner then sat under the stars talking and holding one another. It was then that she shared with me the sexual abuse and trauma she experienced as a child. Learning this, made me sad, mad, and disappointed all at the same time. I was sad for her, mad at her abuser, and disappointed in me even more for not responding the way I should have during the early parts of our marriage.

This woman truly was broken, lost, and confused. I didn't know. I couldn't believe Liyah never shared that with anyone. That's too much for a child to carry alone.

Liyah shared how she started seeing a counselor after I left home, and it was really helping her release the trauma and past pain so that she could embrace the love and possibilities around her.

When I really thought about things concerning this woman, I was simply amazed. Aliyah was strong. She was smart, still talented, and I couldn't believe she was still allowing me the possibility to make her mine.

Things were on the up and up at the church too. Dad Blackwell was allowing me small stepping stones bit by bit back into the music ministry at TBNDC Fellowship Church. I was humble and grateful even for the tiny pieces that he was providing me, considering all that I'd done. The whole experience was humbling to say the very least.

After a year of pure commitment at the church combined with community service, I earned my title of Minister of Music back. I was absolutely ecstatic and had big plans for how we were going to minister in song and in service. I planned to definitely target our young adult group, those individuals who were lost and alone, and those who felt they'd messed up in life too bad that there was no way of escape or point of return. I was confident and certain that was my purpose.

Considering what I'd experienced and had been through, I felt personally lead to this generation of people.

Chapter 19
Beauty for Ashes – Aliyah

Some people were absolutely elated after learning that Josiah and I had entered into the restoration phase of our marriage. In that same manner, there were some people who felt that I was a complete and total, desperate fool for staying with a man who publicly humiliated me by having a baby while we were under a supposed covenant.

Truthfully, I had to learn to ignore it all. My focus was still on my healing and where God was leading me. It's interesting though because a lot of people don't realize the amount of work it takes to both start over alone after a divorce, and to start over when reconciling with your spouse after a broken marriage. It still takes work!

It's a daily process that requires continued forgiveness, trust, and intentionality toward rebuilding. Josiah and I both decided that we wanted to do the work... together! We chose to stand together in forgiveness. Forgiving ourselves of all our past missteps we made as individuals and together. We chose to heal together through the pain, even that which we inflicted on one another.

We decided to stand together against judgement from all of

those that expressed opinion, disgust, or any other feelings about the lives we lived. We elected to grow together in love, agape love to be exact. The Godly unconditional love that allows us to love ourselves and one another as is, regardless of the conditions or circumstances encountered.

Josiah and I opted to prevail against any and all parts of pain, trauma, lies, shame, and destruction the enemy tried to speak over our lives! We focused on pulling one another up and out of the hands of the enemy while running into the arms of the Lord for our healing and victory. We realized we were stronger together and decided to see what blessings God had in store for us within our union.

I not only had to forgive my husband for the pain he caused, I had to forgive myself for being broken, for ignoring my trauma, and for carrying it into my marriage. Honestly, the hardest area to allow forgiveness to flourish was for myself. As I progressed in that area, the healing and forgiveness I needed for Josiah came naturally.

Five years ago, today, I saw nothing but devastation, nothing but brokenness, nothing but sadness, hurt, pain, humiliation, and shame. To date, I see nothing but positive possibilities.

To confirm God's word is true, the young adult ministry has

grown from 150 to 800 members under Josiah and my leadership as co-young adult pastors.

Pastor Blackwell is currently looking at expanding the facility because membership in the church has increased more than 50%.

We also started a new substance abuse counseling program at the church for people struggling with drug and alcohol addiction. We advocated to open a daycare center for any young adults wanting to serve in the church but couldn't commit because they needed a baby sitter. Had it not been for the things that we experienced during that season that caused so much pain, we wouldn't have been able to understand or recognize the need of others.

The test that was externally criticized and judged, activated a new level of wisdom, insight, and authority that was needed for the hundreds of people we later encountered. God was truly in the blessing business. It's pure facts that He is able to do exceedingly, abundantly above all that we ask or think. Oh, before I forget, Josiah also released a project titled, "Eyes Have not Seen." Let me tell you, the song is FIRE! I'm so proud of my baby.

Many people will have their own opinions and judgements

about our journey, but in the end, none of them really matter. What we chose works for us. We chose the path of forgiveness, we chose faith, love, healing, and restoration. When people make comments about how Josiah could forgive me for my brokenness or ask me how I can continue loving a man with a "love child" outside of our marriage, I refer them to Ephesians 4:32, "Be kind and compassionate to one another, forgiving each other, just as in Christ God forgave you."

Josiah and I made a huge mess of things in the beginning, we burned some bridges with each other along the way. In turn, God was able to create something new and beautiful in the place of those ashes that were left from what was burned down.

Little Josiah and his baby brother were inseparable. Their relationship as they grew older became stronger each day. Honestly, I loved it. Some people even had the audacity to ask me how I could love a child that wasn't mine and one who came from such hurtful circumstances.

They asked, "He's a constant reminder of the pain and damage, isn't he?"

I'll be honest, those were fighting words for me. This child did nothing wrong to deserve the disparate and unfair treatment people were referring to.

First and foremost, he is a child of God and second, he is a product of the man that I love. That's how and why I love him like I do. Please believe that's not going to change. And that's bottom line!

So, you've met my man, heard the struggles of our past, and read the real of our test and turnaround. Some wonder how long we'll actually sustain in our marriage being that it has gone through so much trauma.

But you know what they say, "What doesn't kill you, makes you stronger."

I've got an even bigger and better question for you, what happened to Tiffeny? I think I'll let her tell you.

Epilogue – "Tiffeny's Truth"

Yeah, I knew he was married. But my momma always told me, "I don't care what the circumstances are, always go for what you want baby girl. Regardless of who or what barriers may be in the way."

Then she'd kiss me on my forehead. At the time, she was specifically referring to a man. My momma was always referring to a man. Some people coined my momma as homewrecker, hussy, slut, or flat out tramp. These were mainly women of course, but my momma never let that knock her down and she would walk pass everyone with her head held high.

I'm not going to lie, back in the day it used to embarrass and irritate me to no end. As I grew older and lived through my fair share of heartaches provided by this cruel world, I began to understand and relate to my momma more and more, especially after what my dad put her through.

I'm originally from Las Vegas Nevada, the place many people referred to as "Sin City." Vegas stayed poppin' and turnt because there was always so much to do. It made complete and total sense why so many people called it "Sin City."

Even in the suburbs there was always drama and high crime! There were slot machines in the grocery stores and hookers on almost every corner, at the court houses, and in the churches. Paul said it best in Romans 7:21, "I find then a law, that, when I would do good, evil is present with me."

I grew up in a two-parent home for the majority of my childhood until I was about 12 years old. That's when I remember momma and daddy getting into a big fight and daddy left. It was odd though because he left with some man. The memories I have of my momma and daddy being together were almost fairytale like and fictional until recently. I'd forgotten about the constant arguments and verbal jabs they'd make toward one another during dinner. I pictured our home and their marriage being perfect, but I of course, was indisputably in denial about all of it. We stayed in the suburb area of Las Vegas, Nevada but because my momma was a partier, we made frequent visits to the strip on Las Vegas Boulevard in the city that never sleeps. This of course was before she got saved.#

About the Author

Brandy Lynette was born a California girl but now resides in Louisville, KY with her 3 handsome intelligent sons and younger sister.

Before she started writing, she gained experience in various professional endeavors. Brandy holds a Bachelor Degree in Business from California State University San Bernardino and a Master's Degree in Human Resources from Webster University. She has a passionate gift in playwriting, spoken word, and songwriting. Although new to writing books, Brandy is elated to have found her new passionate place of peace writing contemporary novels.

If you want to know when Brandy's next book will come out, please visit her website at http://royalbeeme.com, email and follow her on social media:

Email – LadyBLynette@gmail.com
Instagram - @ladyblynette
Facebook - @brandylynette

Made in the USA
Monee, IL
10 March 2021